More praise for Indu Sundaresan and

IN THE CONVENT OF LITTLE FLOWERS

"Indu Sundaresan guides us through a culture in transition. . . .
The characters are unforgettable. . . . Sundaresan's skill with
language opens the door to India as well as the human heart."

—E. Ethelbert Miller, Director, African American
Resource Center, Howard University

"India, land of fragrances and colors! Indu Sundaresan shows
us these two qualities in a smart way."

—Shahrnush Parsipur, author of *Touba and the Meaning of Night*

THE SPLENDOR OF SILENCE

"Sundaresan unfolds her bittersweet story in flashbacks that
are full of sharply drawn details and adroit dialogue. It's a
riveting read."

—*Seattle Times*

"A sprawling story of forbidden love."

—*Publishers Weekly*

"A colorful, engrossing read."

—*Library Journal*

"Indu Sundaresan expertly blends together history, memorable characters, and the sights, colors, and smells of India to
create a hugely compelling novel. It is, quite literally, a feast
for the senses."

—David Davidar, internationally bestselling author of
mperors

D1040576

"Finely researched and full of evocative details, this sweeping tale of intrigue brings to life a fascinating era with richly drawn characters and a story that is engrossing, deep, and surprising."

—Samina Ali, author of *Madras on Rainy Days*

These titles are also available as eBooks

In the
Convent
of
Little Flowers

INDU SUNDARESAN

WASHINGTON SQUARE PRESS
NEW YORK   LONDON   TORONTO   SYDNEY

Washington Square Press
A Division of Simon & Schuster, Inc.
1230 Avenue of the Americas
New York, NY 10020

First Washington Square Press trade paperback edition September 2009

WASHINGTON SQUARE PRESS and colophon are trademarks of
Simon & Schuster, Inc.

For information about special discounts for bulk purchases,
please contact Simon & Schuster Special Sales at
1-866-506-1949 or business@simonandschuster.com.

The Simon & Schuster Speakers Bureau can bring authors to your live
event. For more information or to book an event contact the
Simon & Schuster Speakers Bureau at 1-866-248-3049 or visit our
website at www.simonspeakers.com.

"Shelter of Rain" was first published in *The Vincent Brothers Review* (2000).
"Bedside Dreams" was published in *India Currents* (November 2004) and
Verve magazine (India, July–August 2005). "The Faithful Wife" was first
published in *The Pen and the Key: 50th Anniversary Anthology of Pacific
Northwest Writers* (2005).

Designed by Jill Putorti

Manufactured in the United States of America

10 9 8 7 6 5 4 3 2 1

The Library of Congress Cataloging-in-Publication Data for the
hardcover is available.

ISBN 978-1-4165-8610-4 (pbk)
ISBN 978-1-4165-8618-0 (ebook)

For Sitara
Who lights up my life

In the
Convent
of
Little Flowers

Shelter of Rain

In my childhood
Deep equator skies
Whitened by an unforgiving sun
I stand now
Under the shelter of rain

I arrive at SeaTac airport early, two hours ahead of time. The terminal is deserted now, with yawning, shiny seats. After I sit, a little girl and her mother come to settle across from me, although empty places stretch to the far corner and, I think, around. The girl carries a sand bucket, which she sets down on the well-trodden carpet. Then, with a spade, she scoops imaginary sand in and out of the bucket. I watch the child's face, her cheeks puffed in whistleless concentration, her hair cut in little-girl bangs, her arms sturdy in a summer frock's sleeves. I was once like this girl—but also so different. I played in the red earth under the shade of a banyan tree, the mud coloring my palms for weeks. I had forgotten those days. But the letter came out of nowhere, with no warning, to remind me.

As I shift in my seat, the letter crackles against my leg. I take it out of my jeans pocket and smooth it over a knee. The paper is rough, unfinished, torn out of a child's handwriting practice notebook; there are sets of four lines throughout the page, the top and bottom ones red, the inner two blue. It has been so long, yet I remember the exhortations to fit capital letters between the red lines and small letters between the blue. That was how, all those years ago, I learned to write. I look again at the paper, and the blue ink swarming over the page swims into a haze.

Since the letter came a month ago, I have thought of nothing else. An envelope blue as my mother Diana's gaze lay on the kitchen counter for that time. In it, looped in an old, educated hand, words blurring before my now often-tired eyes, there is the story of another mother. The letter says *she* gave birth to me, not Diana. She lies sick in her house on Chinglepet street in Chennai.

A map of India has taken up permanent residence on the dining table at home. I could see the map through the corner of my eye no matter what room I was in. I knew I came from that country, twenty-three years ago, but I had not known from where. The letter told me where. It came from the Convent of Little Flowers in Chennai.

We have always had beautiful young girls here. Girls whose mothers could not keep them, dear Padmini. I hope that is still your name. It means the lotus flower. All our little girls have been named thus, after flowers.

You came to us with that name. Your mother gave
you the name. I am sure you have grown up to be as
beautiful as the serene lotus in a village pond.

Tears come each time I read those lines. How dare she—
Sister Mary Theresa—write me after so many years? I was
six when Tom and Diana Merrick took me from the Convent of Little Flowers. They have never been back to India
since. And neither have I. Now I am no longer that child
who left.

There is a faded black-and-white picture in one of Mom's
photo albums. Diana, I mean, not the woman on Chinglepet
street. In it I stand with an expression so scared, so beaten,
I cannot recognize myself. The picture was taken two weeks
before I left India. My feet are bare, my hair in a braid swings
over one skinny shoulder, a new white frock sprayed with
purple flowers billows over my knees. I remember I hated the
day of the year when the frocks came. I do not look at that
picture very often. And yet this Sister Mary Theresa, Mother
Superior, talks of it and brings back the sun-drenched mud
courtyard in the shadow of the Gemini bridge.

Your mother would send frocks for you on every
birthday. Somehow, she always knew the right size.
For your sixth birthday it was a sleeveless white frock
printed with purple lilacs. Have you seen a lilac
blossom, Padmini? Your mother liked flowers. Believe
me, the dress each year was more than she could afford

to do then. Her circumstances had changed, questions would have been asked, but she was brave, she always remembered.

I volunteered to go on call every week after the letter came. My colleagues stared at me in disbelief at first, then escaped thankfully to their suntan lotions and backyards. But I did not care. If I was going to stay awake anyway through the July nights, I might as well keep my mind numbingly occupied. The ER at Harborview is not the place for dreaming of old memories, just brief stunning reflections of how stupid people can get when it comes to injuring themselves. I spent eight hours in surgery one memorable day trying to stitch a twenty-three-year-old man's hand back to his forearm while across the table from me, the ophthalmologist on call worked in tandem on his blown-out right eye. He had tried to pick up a lit cherry bomb.

Yet for me, there was always time to think of the letter. My mother always remembered, Mary Theresa says. But she never remembered to visit. Did she ever come? Did I know her when she came? Or did she just stand on the white-washed verandah and watch me play under the shade of the many-armed banyan in the courtyard?

That memory comes back too. One I do not want. One I try to hold away. But once dredged up, it is here to stay. Why did that letter come? Damn Sister Mary Interfering Theresa. I suddenly remember her too. Short—even to a child she seemed so—with kind black eyes behind thick glasses. *Soda Booddies,* we used to call them. Soda bottle glasses, disfigured by thickness. Mary Theresa had a plump face, spotted by an unrepentant and errant not-yet-eradicated smallpox. Yet her starched white wimple and her wide smile and her gentle hands that never held the neem tree–child-beating branch made us oblivious to it. But we talked under that banyan. She must have joined the convent because no man would marry her. A smallpox-pitted face is not exactly marriage market material. She was also dark. Even as six-year-olds we knew those things. What a pity, we would think, she would have made a wonderful mother. And we would turn yearning glances to the verandah when she appeared, each of us thinking, make me your child, don't be mother to *everyone.*

Sometimes Mary Theresa would walk down the verandah doing her day's work. Sometimes—very often, actually—she would stand with a woman or a man from the outside and point toward our group, or another one. We were far enough away not to know whom she was pointing at. But we knew that man or woman was either one of our parents or a relative come to see us, or, as we often hoped, someone who would make us theirs. It would be a bizarre game for us, watching these people—perhaps related to us by blood, perhaps judging us as their future children—trying to guess whom they belonged to. Sister Mary says my mother always remembered. Did she also come to stand on that verandah? Which one was she?

It never bothered me then. I wonder why it bothers me

now. No one has pointed at me for twenty-three years from across a dusty courtyard.

I came away from that hot city to rainy green Seattle. Tom and Diana lived in a golden western sun–lit condo on Queen Anne Hill. Everything about those three words excited me. Queen. I had seen pictures of one. Anne. The name of a queen. And hill. I had not seen a hill before. Chennai, Mary Theresa tells me now, is flat. I had not seen mountains feathered with wayward snow on October evenings. I had not seen the sun set behind the Olympics or the ferry making its lone streaking way through the calm Puget Sound. Or Mount Rainier, glorious godly Mount Rainier, suddenly appearing on the horizon. For months, I knelt before the windows of our home (how easily the *our* comes now) and watched the sun set each day. I remember Dad, shattered in Vietnam—not from bodily harm—yelling out at night and Mom soothing, crooning, holding him in her arms, lit by the streetlight outside the windows. I would stand at the door to their room and watch until they called me to their bed to lie between them. Until then I had only seen little flowers cry at night, not grown men.

My life since has been peppered by Seattle rain. Rain in the winter—hardly had that in Chennai—rain in the spring, and summer and fall. Chennai is very close to the equator. It must be hot. I remember now it *is* hot. Is that why I love the rain?

I did not choose this life. I did not even choose to be born, let alone to this nameless woman in the southeast corner of India. I did not choose to be given away, or be taken by the sunny blond couple who stood on the verandah one day and, I think, pointed at me. But they took me. I came here. I belong no more to Chinglepet street.

I don't think I have ever realized I am different. I cannot say not American, because what really *is* American? But I look into the mirror more often now and I see that dark skin. To me it seems as dark as Sister Mary Theresa's, yet I am married where she took the veil for hers. *Autre temps, autre moeurs.* Sister Bloody Mary Theresa. I am so angry I will not even now allow her the luxury of having chosen then a life for the love of her religion, for the love of her God, or even, for the love of her work. It must be because somebody rejected her. Or she would not be a nun at the Convent of Little Flowers. And I would not have met her, and she would not have now written me the letter.

Do you remember much of us, dear Padmini? The convent was built in the shadow of the Gemini Flyover, the only road bridge in all of Chennai then, and a big landmark for giving directions. I have seen pictures of America. There are many many such flyovers there. Some even in the shape of clover leaves. But this you must know, these you must have seen. I'm afraid nothing much grows even now in our courtyard. It is still the same, a bare maidan, *dusty when the rains do not come; but under the banyan it is shady. The tree has added a few more arms to the ground since you were last*

here. Every day I stand on the verandah and watch the
children play under its shade and thank God it is still
there. Somehow, it finds the strength to survive year after
year of drought as the trees and saplings around the city
wilt and die. It has been five years since an adequate
rain has visited Chennai.

The lowering skies have now completely engulfed the Cascades outside the floor-to-ceiling glass of the airport. I want to send them westward, across the vast Pacific Ocean, flying over Hawaii, over Hong Kong and Singapore and China, sweeping down the Bay of Bengal to hover over the Gemini Flyover. We have enough rain here. The little flowers could do with some of ours. When she writes like this, in her singsong talking voice, I can remember her even more.

The Merricks came one rain-threatening day to stand on the verandah to choose me. Later Mom would say they brought the rain from Seattle. I firmly believe it was me they wanted among all others. Mom said so, night after night when I asked her. I could barely speak English when I came here, just a few words. It was a long plane ride from Chennai to Seattle. I sat between them in the white frock I hated. They had brought jeans for me, but only boys wore pants; why would I all of a sudden? Besides, the frock was the only thing then that was mine. Under it I wore a baggy pair of Mom's stockings, pooling around my ankles in frothy beige, knotted and pinned at my waist. One of Dad's sweaters flopped over my shoulders down to my knees. Somehow, in giving me their clothes, they made me theirs. They patted me a lot during that flight, not knowing what to say. They would pat me on the head, on the shoulders, on the knees, all accompanied by a stream of gibberish. English, I found out later. I dutifully nodded my head and chewed on unforgiving limp lettuce and candy bars. I had not tasted chocolate till then. I still like it. I guess the flight was not so bad after all.

School was hard. At the Convent of Little Flowers we had our classes in a haphazard fashion. It depended on how free Sister Mary was during the day. She taught us math and English (not very well, obviously). A schoolmaster came in for Tamil. Strangely, I remember him very well. He was a handsome man, with a commanding movie-star mustache and a deep male voice. At the Convent of Little Flowers, we were all either little flowers or older women—teachers and sweepers and clerks. The schoolmaster was a welcome distraction, despite his polio-affected limp that made him swing to one side as he walked. As we forgot Sister Mary's smallpox face, we forgot the schoolmaster's polio walk. With the precocity of children left to themselves most of the day, we made up happy endings for Sister Mary and the schoolmaster. It did not matter that one was a nun and the other married.

For my first day at Coe Elementary, sometime in mid-October, Dad took the morning off from work and the three of us walked down the road together to school. They insisted upon holding my hands. I let them. It was a nice feeling. The first person we met was Mrs. Haley, my class teacher, with her triangular glasses and her formfitting sweater dress and her short cropped hair artfully arranged in curls around her head. I asked her, my English still not strong, if she was married. She was. She was most unlike Sister Mary. Then I thought it was the glasses that did it. It was the glasses anyway that made me unclench my hand from Dad's large one and willingly put it in hers, and for many hours in the next few months I would stare at Mrs. Haley's pretty face in class. She was never as pretty as Mom, though.

That first day she took me into class, to the very front, and said, "Class, this is Padmini Merrick. Everyone, please welcome Padmini to the class." The class promptly chorused back, "Welcome, Pud-mi-ni." There was one little boy in front who yelled out the loudest, Mike. Even then I thought him quite handsome with his brown hair and hazel eyes and two front teeth knocked out in a schoolyard brawl. For many months after that Mike would fight for me when someone teased me about my accent, or the English I learned painfully at first and then rapidly, or for sitting quietly in the schoolyard in May as the plum and peach trees burst into wondrous pink and white blossoms. The banyan seemed to be always green; I don't remember flowers in the Convent of Little Flowers. A week ago Mike told me what he thought when he first saw me standing in front of the class.

We were sitting on the park benches on Pier 66 a few minutes before sunset. It had been a warm day and there were people all around us, laughing and talking and feeding the persistent gulls. "You were wearing a red sweater and black jeans," Mike said. I was. Funny he would remember that; he never seems to notice what I wear now. "But," he continued, "I mostly see in my mind a thin face with deep black eyes, huge and frightened. Your hair was long and braided down your back to the waist. You cut it in fourth grade, I remember that too."

I had not seen many boys until then, only little flower girls. So I was fascinated by Mike with his blown-out front teeth—which he showed endearingly each time he smiled—and his spiky hair, and his dirty hands and face. Over the years that face has changed only slightly. I think I must have known I would marry Mike one day, because I don't remember having seen anyone but him in all the years of my memory.

Are you married now, dear Padmini? Do you work? I hear that in America all women work. Do you have children of your own, Padmini? Who did you marry? Is he Indian? American? So many questions to ask of you. So many things I want to know. Not just for myself, child, but for another person who asks after you. I have told you of your mother, who wishes she might see you now that she is sick. She has uterine cancer and has undergone months of chemotherapy and radiation. She is very brave really; she bears her pain and her nausea with a strength I would not have attributed to her. She does not talk about you, but I know she thinks and wonders where you are. I know

her well, your mother. I knew she always wanted you
but could not keep you for various reasons. Reasons I
will not go into here.

Why? I want to cry out each time I read that. She talks of knowing my mother, of being next to her and not hearing her ask after me. Why does Meddling Sister Mary Theresa care what has happened to me when my own mother—no, the woman who gave birth to me—does not seem to care? And why does she want to know if I have children? Mike and I have none, not yet at least. Somehow, my memory fills with pictures of little flowers who have no parents. But I think at times I would like a boy with spiky hair who fights ferociously for what he thinks is right . . . or a girl just like him—like Mike.

I called Mom when the letter came. They live in Bellingham now; Dad is retired from Boeing. They have a tiny cottage on four acres of land, spilling into the Pacific at the edge of the garden. I think it was living on Queen Anne that made them want the space. So they gave Mike and me the condo and went to their little house up north. Dad is still too young to be retired, but he wanted to stop working and potter about a garden, his own for once. Mom works now in the administrative offices of Western; she says it drives her nuts to have Dad home all the time, pestering her about something or the other. Dee, get me the wheelbarrow; Dee, are you sure the spaghetti isn't overcooked? Dee, when is Padma going to visit? He won't pick up the phone and ask me; he will just pester Mom until she does.

They called me Padma from when I came to them. When the letter came, I asked Mom why they did that, when my name was Padmini. Padma also meant lotus, Mom said, and they asked Sister Mary Theresa for a nickname, a shorter form of Padmini. They did not know Tamil well enough to do so themselves. Looking back, it was a peculiar conversation. We were almost like strangers with each other again, afraid to say anything outright, filling up silences with thoughts. We talked of my name, of Mary Theresa; I read out parts of the letter to her. To them both. Dad had picked up the extension as he always did when I called, but he did not say a word until the very last. I just heard his presence on the other end. Then gently, his voice cracking, he said, "Padma, are you going to India?" I had to say I didn't know. Then he said, "I have to go now, sweetheart, the dandelions are growing even as we speak." After Dad put down the extension, I asked Mom a question I had not asked for a long time. It had not been necessary to do so, but now it suddenly was. "Mom, was it *me* you wanted from the Convent of Little Flowers?" And she answered as she always did: "Only you, my dear, no one else. Ever."

I used to be fascinated by my parents at the beginning. I would sit on Dad's lap and stare into his eyes, blue as the midsummer sky on a breathless morning. Then I saw the lines around his mouth, which showed he smiled a lot. I hung from his arm with my knees swinging off the ground. Mom brought me milk in the mornings; no one had done that for me before. I learned to sleep in my own bed, without fleeing across the hall to theirs in the middle of the night, knowing I would wake them. And I learned to be fiercely protective of them, and jealous if they bent down to talk with the neighbor's child. They were mine, I thought. And so I filled in pieces like a jigsaw, a history of my own with Mom and Dad, without the little flowers.

We do not usually keep in touch with our little flowers, dear Padmini, yet here I am writing to you. When the Merricks came to the convent looking for a little girl, I judged them very carefully. I was still very young then, perhaps I did not seem so to you, but I watched them, I listened, I heard the kindness in their voices and saw it in their eyes. I knew they would be good for you. Did I make a good choice, my child?

I should not say however that the choice was entirely mine. When Tom and Diana Merrick came to the Convent of Little Flowers they wanted a child younger than one year. Later, I took them out onto the verandah to show them the school and the mess hall and the playground behind. You were playing hide-and-seek with your friends between the arms of the banyan. You were the seeker and as you danced your way through the tree roots, you were singing. I cannot remember anymore what the song was; it was in Tamil. Even for a child you had a haunting, lilting voice. Diana Merrick wanted you then, just as you

*were, your hair sticking to your head in sweaty strips,
your arms and legs dusty to the elbows and knees, your
bare feet the color of mud.*

*It wrenched my heart to give you away. But they
insisted. No other child would do, not even the one
picked out ahead of time. I said yes after four weeks of
pleading from them. Four weeks when I watched and
listened and decided they would love you as much as I
do. Have they been good to you, my dear?*

Why the hell did she give me away if it wrenched her
heart? And yet how could anyone but Tom and Diana be
Mom and Dad? It has been a month since the letter came,
but they have not come down to visit. Every week, Mom and
Dad used to pop by on some pretext on Sundays for lunch.
Oh, we were in the neighborhood. Your dad wanted to shop
at a downtown store, nothing else would do. (Dad has, to
my knowledge, never been in what he calls "fancy stores,"
and neither has Mom.) Or the fresh vegetables at Pike Place
beckoned to them all the way from Bellingham, where they
grow at least half an acre of vegetables in their garden—and
give away crates of carrots and cauliflowers under a FREE sign
at the top of their driveway.

But they have not come down in four weekends. I have
been on call, at work; that was my excuse. They rapidly grow
old waiting for me to do whatever I want to do. If I could
burn the letter and flush the ashes and it would all disappear

in the toilet water, perhaps I would do that. But then I would not be here at SeaTac, waiting for the flight to arrive from L.A. I looked up the route. Chennai to London, London to New York, New York to L.A., and then here. Exactly twenty-four hours in flight. The least I could do was come here two hours ahead of scheduled arrival. I sit at the gate now, staring through the Plexiglas as the cleaning crew, the catering crew, the refueling crew, the baggage-handlers, the tire-pressure-checking crew all buzz around some airplane, swarming into it and then popping out at odd places.

The letter is folded inside my jeans pocket. I wear pants now.

Tom Merrick showed me his citation for the Vietnam war. He said he was wounded in it and decorated for bravery. I don't quite remember what the incident was, dear Padmini, no doubt you do. He must have talked to you about it. But when he told me, I wasn't listening to his words, just the tone of his voice. Here was a man who would be kind to my little Padmini, I thought. Have they been kind?

It has been twenty-three years, yet I feel as though I know what you look like. You must have your mother's looks. She has always been a beautiful woman; even now, when the cancer has ravaged her, she has an ethereal beauty, a charm of manner. Her children think so, and I agree with them.

That kills me each time I read it. She had time for other children, not just one more, mind you, *children*. Why did she not keep me? Sister Mary Bloody Theresa.

> *Yes, I know your mother well. As well as I know myself. You see, we were born to the same house, the same mother. Your mother is my little sister. She has always been somewhat young, somewhat petted. Your birth was unexpected. Enough said. I had found my calling before you were born, if I hadn't I would gladly have taken you. As it turns out, I did take you, in another capacity. And perhaps you would have known me well these last twenty-three years if the Merricks had not come that day to the convent. But, everything happens for a reason. If the smallpox had not visited me and left its mark, I might have married . . . I might be married anyway, there was a man. But . . . things did not work out. I changed my name from Chandra to Sister Mary Theresa. When I was converted, they asked where I would like to do God's work and I said it would be at an orphanage, at the Convent of Little Flowers. A year later, you came to me as a baby. But do not worry, your mother married well. The indiscretion was forgotten, not made public, anyway.*

This is when I hate her the most. Bloody Sister Mary Theresa. How easily I was forgotten. How easily I was made an "indiscretion," how well my mother married because she was young and pretty and fair, Mary Theresa tells me. I don't feel sympathy for the woman lying sick on Chinglepet street. She has her other children. I have never been her child. Even now, it is Sister Mary Theresa who writes.

> *In another world I would be your perima. Your Chandra perima. It means "Big Mother." As your mother's older sister, I am your mother too. Oh, Padmini, have I done right by you? Do not ever think I forgot, or didn't know where you were. I knew. Just as I have known where to write now. And I write to ask this. May I come to see you? There is a conference of Catholic nuns in Seattle, imagine me coming to your hometown! I am not very old yet, but life tires me now. I cannot even look after your mother very well, for the duties at the orphanage weigh me down. But I do want to see that I fulfilled the responsibility your mother gave me. Would you like to see your perima, my dear Padmini?*

A brief, stunning thought comes now. The frock in cheap cotton that came every birthday, was it Sister Mary Theresa who sent them? I have a sudden vision of a nun in a dimly lit shop, peering nearsightedly over bales of garish cotton, giving away two or three ill-afforded rupees for a few square centimeters of cloth. Then she would have gone to the tailor and put out a hand from the floor, measuring me for him.

This tall. Only this thin. The frocks never fit. For her, I was always taller and fatter than I actually was. She saw me as a mother would. And she let me go to a better life, away from her, as only a mother could.

I have wondered why Mom and Dad went to India. I asked Mom once. It was Vietnam, she said. Dad had done his tour of duty three years before India, but it stayed with him. So they went back for a vacation to that corner of the world, drawn to the mysticism, the history, even the peace in India, in search of something . . . and came back with a daughter. They never had more children. I did not ask why.

I have come alone to SeaTac. Now the terminal is hissing with muted conversation. It has started to rain. Again. The lights have become brighter inside; outside the tarmac glistens wet, and airplanes have their windshield wipers on. The little girl with the sand bucket and her mother are long gone, where I do not know. I did not notice them leave. I think only of *her*.

I wonder what she will be like. My *perima*. I am to find out in two minutes. The plane landed and nosed its way to the gate a short while ago. As the people pour out of the doors I stand at one corner and look for her. And I see her. I had not realized she was so short or that a nun's habit could look the same after twenty-three years. I should have known she would even travel in her habit. *Perima*. I roll the word around in my mind. No, to me she will always be Sister Mary Theresa. But I am suddenly glad we belong together. I stare at her. Fatigue creases her skin, and she walks a tired walk. Just then, she sees me too and smiles. It is a shy smile, a wonderful smile. She will meet Mike today. Tomorrow, I will take her to Bellingham to meet Mom and Dad. I think they will like her. I do. Already.

She comes up to me and holds out her hand. I clutch it wordlessly; even tears will not come now. *Padmini, I am so glad you kept your name.* That smile again. I think I have always known this beautiful woman with her smallpox-marked face.

It is just like my face, after all.

Three and a Half Seconds

<hr />

*A*t first there is no sensation, no feeling at all, not even fear. Just an intense, heart-filled longing for freedom. Then strangely it is peaceful, no remorse at leaving behind the old life and stepping into the new. Meha laughs out loud, listening to the sound of her voice echo down the well of balconies. But no one wakes in the flats. No lights come on, no heads stick out of windows, no fists are shaken in disgust. They all still sleep. Tomorrow they will know, Meha thinks. Tomorrow they will see what Chandar and she have done. Time enough for that.

This really started when Bikaner had formed as a bud in her forty-one years ago. Meha had been married six months, her tummy was still flat, she did not yet gag at the sight of food or run out into the fields to retch, and as each additional month passed the questions rose around her in a forest of whispers, buzzing louder every day.

"What, no good news?" or "Are you not being a good wife?" or later, more boldly, "Lie back and let him do it—think good thoughts and a son will be born."

No one dared talk with Chandar, of course. As Meha told him of each question, as worry drew lines on her young forehead, Chandar would take her slim hands in his, kiss the upturned palms, and say, "Ignore them, *jaaneman,* what do they know? What do we care?"

Six months and a tiny shiver still thrilled her spine when Chandar called her *jaaneman.* She was his life, his very mind. They knew each other better than anyone else in their lives. It was as though their childhood, their adolescence, all those who peopled their lives—parents and village teachers, uncles and aunts and cousins—had vanished in this haze of marital love. Yet a month before the wedding, they were to each other just names on horoscopes that matched perfectly.

The stars had decreed that they were ideal mates before they even met. At night, when the small kerosene lamp in the corner burned low and pungent, they talked as though they were children learning to talk; they touched as though seeing through blind eyes. A hundred different forms of love, all hidden from the outside world. In the other room—the only other room of the two-room hut—lived Chandar's parents and his younger brothers.

Meha's hands still glowed with the honey-orange whorls and curls of henna; her mother-in-law had told her to not let the colors fade for a whole year. So one evening each month she sat by the lamp and piped little lines of henna paste over her wedding design. The in-laws watched approvingly—here was a daughter-in-law who did not expect to sit around all day while her henna dried; instead she wore it at night. They did not know what Meha knew: although she could not touch Chandar for fear of smearing the patterns on her hands, he could touch her.

Half a second.

When Meha came to the family as a bride she was first ushered to the room that was to be theirs, freshly added to the hut. Four mud walls, a swept-earth floor, and a dry palm thatch on the roof through which in the mornings a sun mosaic beckoned her to rise. The walls were slathered with cow dung, and the sweet-sickly smell, mixed with the aroma of hay, still drifted around in slow circles. There was no furniture other than a new *charpai,* its knitted jute bed taut in the wooden frame, a printed handloom sheet thrown over it. Both were part of Meha's dowry. The *charpai* was newly strung, its ropes springy. Over time it would sag in the middle, scooping out the shapes of their bodies. On that single *charpai* she sat and waited, watching her hennaed hands clasped around her knees, tinkling the gold and red glass bangles around her wrist, something much like anxiety gripping her body. What would he be like, this man she had married? It seemed like a long wait for a man who was to share her life from now on, from whom she would never be parted, whose face she had barely seen.

Chandar had come to her in exquisite kindness, lifting her veil, touching her face with gentle hands, saying simply, "Welcome to my life, *jaaneman*."

It was a line from a Hindi film song that Meha herself used to hum. She had not seen the movie, but the chai shopkeeper's transistor blared the music every day. When he used those words, her panic fled. Still she could not lift her head to look at him. But she knew then that they would always be together, that they were meant to be.

It is strange what events come to mind after forty-two years of marriage. And now of all times, when there seems to be so little time, she remembers a girl from her father's village who had been married before her. She cannot remember her name, but she remembers other things about her.

That girl had gone to her *maikai* in a bullock cart, head bowed under her wedding veil, face wreathed with fearful smiles in anticipation of her new home. She had come back to visit her parents a month later. She had grown thin, sullen, though she still smiled, proud of her new status of wifehood. Yet no one in Meha's village failed to see the welts that swelled in vertical lines where her back was bared between her blouse and the bottom half of her sari.

★ ★ ★

But it had never been like that for her, Meha thinks. There had never been scars to cover . . . until now.

Chandar's family, like Meha's, owned land in the southern part of the state. Five acres. And from that land came sustenance for them all. Each spring, the two white bullocks painstakingly plowed up great big clods of earth, a minor eruption from beneath. The lumps of earth were then hammered into smaller pieces with wooden mallets and stones. The whole family worked in the merciless sun: the men, bareheaded—for their turbans would slip off as they bent—and the women with sari *pallus* drawn over their foreheads. Each spring the dry, cracked overwinter fields powdered beneath their hands. Five acres can be large to mere human hands. But this did not deter them. This was their work, this was their life. The bullocks, their neck skins pendant like an old woman's jowls, were hitched to a wheel in the well. With each turn, buffalo-hide buckets brought up water and tipped it into a channel. The water swirled through its muddy walls to the fields—at first soaking through the thirsty earth; then, as though sated, the earth spewed up the water, flooding the fields. Rice saplings toted in reed-woven baskets were planted in this standing water.

Meha's arms darkened to the sleeves of her blouse. Her sari hiked up about her knees, the *pallu* wrapped around her thick black hair, she bent over the field each day. She would clutch a rice shoot and plunge her hand into the watery earth. Her fingers dug deep through the soil, leaving a single, green rice sapling standing in their place. Then came long days of weeding the field, and watching it grow strong and lush. Toward September, thick golden rice buds encrusted the ends of the stalks.

There were lazy days too. A raised platform was built in the field; and here, under a cloth canopy to shield them from the heat, Meha and Chandar would lie and talk. Every now and then, they would lift their heads to yell at errant sparrows picking at their precious rice. They were human scarecrows. And here, when the sun hung in glaring shimmers around the ripening rice, Bikaner was conceived. They had little else to do, and it was early days yet in their marriage.

The questions, the snickers, the looks in the village stopped as Meha's stomach grew. Nine months later, one sweltering June afternoon, Meha dragged herself to the shelter of a copper pod tree and gave birth to her son.

Meha looks down at the concrete pavement below. The flats ring this courtyard, their balconies fronting one another. Mrs. Patel left her bra out as usual on the clothesline, confident no one would steal it fourteen stories up from the ground. It is taking so long, this journey of retrospection. It is taking so long that there is even time to remember incidents from her childhood. Fifty-five years ago. The memories come clear as water, as though they happened yesterday. On her graying head, Meha can feel the pull of fingers as her mother plaited her hair each morning.

★ ★ ★

And during that daily ritual her mother told her stories of strong women. Of the goddess Parvati who, when she was bored and needed a distraction, made Lord Ganesha from within herself, without her husband or any other man. Who turned into Kali when her husband came home from the war and found a "son" guarding the door to his palace; a son he did not know existed, a son whom he killed, angering his powerful wife. Kali, almost demented in her grief, started wrecking the world and no one could stop her, not even her husband, Lord Shiva. So the gods appeased her by giving back life to Ganesha with a new elephant head to replace the one his father had cut off. And so Meha learned the power of a mother.

Her maternal instincts were carefully cultivated in an ancient society attuned to motherhood. The stories told her that even husbands were not important. Not dispensable, but not really important. The child was everything. She did all that was required of her. But when Bikaner came, there was only a gap where nature should have fostered love.

One second.

From the beginning he was a demanding child, greedily gulping at her breast, screaming if not attended to. She had looked at him in astonishment; had her body made this little thing? But no matter what she thought, the lessons of her childhood were well learned. It was her duty, her responsibility. So she cooed to him, held him against her, never denied him her breast, indulged him. Sometimes she did this because it was expected of her, sometimes because after all he was the result of her love for Chandar.

But Chandar also looked at him with surprise. Oh, he patted him to sleep when he cried at night (even though this was supposed to be woman's work), but in him was the same void that Meha felt. They glanced at each other thoughtfully during those first months after Bikaner's birth, both knowing they had had him because the village wanted them to, both also aware that life would not have been intolerable if the child were not there. They never talked about it, they just knew.

Beside her Meha can see Chandar and wants to reach out to touch his forehead. She wants to pull him to her for a kiss. Like when they were young and he would lie against her, his head tucked under her chin, listening to the steady beat of her heart. When she puts out her hand, she comes up with only air. He is too far away, but as though he understands her need, he looks at her and smiles. For Meha that is enough.

Almost as if he sensed their distance, Bikaner grew more demanding as the years passed. They tried very hard to love him. But he was a cruel child, given to destroying sparrows' nests, using a slingshot on squirrels. All children were cruel, Meha thought. They did things heedless of consequences. Then one day she came upon him beating a stray monkey.

The monkeys haunted the Hanuman temple's compound in the village, begging for bananas and coconut wedges from the pilgrims. They swarmed over the branches of a banyan tree, their bodies a mass of silver-gray fur, their eyes bright and ringed in black. Every now and then, a child would fall from its mother's grip as she swung through the tree, only to scramble up the trunk on shaky limbs. One of these, Bikaner, then only five, had brought home. He had tied its hands together with a piece of twine and weighted the other end with a large rock. The monkey could move around, but only in tight little circles around the rock. The family was at the fields that afternoon and Meha had returned home to get water for them. The monkey's squeals drew her to the courtyard. There she saw Bikaner lift his stick and bring it down on the little animal over and over again. When she arrived, it was too bloody and broken to even whimper, too far gone to be saved. It just lay on the ground, hands up over its eyes to cover its face, humanlike in its gestures. She pulled a frenzied Bikaner away from the monkey, yanked the stick from him, and cleaned the blood off his face, hands, and clothes. Then she slapped him, hard, leaving the imprint of her fingers on his face. She could not bring herself to say anything to Bikaner; speech was impossible, she just slapped him and walked away, her heart exploding in her chest.

That night, Chandar buried the monkey in the fields behind the hut. They told no one of the incident; the in-laws never knew. Chandar came back from the fields and leaned his spade against the mud wall of the courtyard. Meha glanced at him and he nodded. Then he washed his hands and sat down near the men of the family to smoke a hand-rolled *beedi*. They stared at each other for a long time that night, the squeals of children, the low murmur of women's voices, and the harsher sounds of men's laughter melting away. They were no longer newlyweds; it was not their turn to sleep in the room, so they slept outside in the courtyard with everyone else. There had been no time to talk. So they had not talked.

That night, and for many nights that followed, Bikaner had stayed up wailing, keeping the whole family at the edge of sleep. Meha tried to comfort him, but she was too disgusted, too ashamed of this child she had borne. When they went to the temple, Bikaner would stay under the banyan, watching the chattering monkeys with a stolid, unwavering gaze. He would stare at the little monkeys until Meha pulled him away.

And so time had passed. They had both ignored Bikaner's cruelty. It seemed easier to do so as any alternative was immensely frightening. Confront it, they could not. What to say to a five-year-old child? How to say it? Meha looks at Chandar now, wondering if there is time to remind him of that incident. It has lain gathering cobwebs in their minds. Yet now, dusted off and held to her gaze again, Meha realizes that they should have seen that this predicament too would eventually have come. They should never have forgotten the monkey's death. They should have done something about the monkey's death.

One year, not long after that, the rains failed. The irrigation canals dried up as the well emptied, water lying low in its depths. Meha threw stones down the well and listened for a long time before they hit the bottom. The five hard-worked acres lay dry and fractured. The next year it rained, but barely enough to wet the scorch ed earth. They dipped into their reserves of rice and wheat. The huge grain silo in the main room of the hut rang hollow as the children played inside it. The four large copper pod trees outside the hut that sheltered the family from the sun now played host to vultures sitting solemnly on the lower branches, eyeing the children with hungry glances.

Some of the goats and cows sickened and died. The pariah dogs fought for *chappatis* with the children. Chandar and his brothers sat around in the courtyard on their haunches, watching the cloudless sky with worried eyes, watching as the days passed and the small transistor radio crackled with news of the worst drought in a hundred years. When Meha found the time, she sat by Chandar, not too close to him because they were in public, but close enough to share in his onerous anxiety. He said once, "Why did your father ever agree to give you to me?"

Meha laughed. They had been married eight years. "He would not take me back now," she said. "Not after all this time; I'm too old now." She put love into her voice. "Things will improve, Chandar."

He shook his head and looked down at his hands, callused from years of working in the fields, his nails cracked and chipped. Then he squinted up at the sun again, burning down upon them, harsh and searing.

They ate the goats that week, chewing on stringy muscle and brittle bones—even the marrow seemed to have dried up. The cows watched mournfully, but they could not bring themselves to eat the cows. Good Hindus did not. So the cows were left to die outside the compound wall; during the day vultures, crows, flies—and at night a liver-colored jackal—stripped their bones of meat. It was the end of their existence as farmers; they all knew this. Two consecutive years of drought had devastated them. Without the animals there could be no farming, without water they were as good as dead.

Meha went hungry for days, using her share of food for Chandar, too weak to scold him when he gave a morsel to the pariah dog that haunted their compound.

Meha touches her wrist lightly. There is almost no muscle left, just skin covering aged bones. Just as in those days in the village, so many years ago. The government promised aid; they even brought food packets to the villages. Rice, some dal, *a few saris and dhotis to cover dried-up bodies. That lasted only for a few months, in the end, the government gave up. Even they could not conjure rain-filled clouds to placate a thirsty earth. But then, Chandar and she had been young, resilient, confident even.*

Chandar finally decided that they must head to the big city in search of work. And so they packed their belongings: one extra set of clothes each, which was all they had; a handful of rice; four handfuls of *atta* from the communal bin to knead for *chappatis;* a brass pot; an old pink talcum powder tin with the top cut off and filled with chili pickle; fifty rupees rolled into a tight wad and tied to the *pallu* of Meha's sari. Chandar's parents left the land with other sons. He promised to send them money, even to send for them when there was money. For now it was only Meha and Chandar. And Bikaner.

The bus journey to the outskirts of Mumbai took up half their money—a little of the rest went for food at a street corner *panipuri* stand.

Meha can remember being horrified at paying five rupees for the panipuri. *They must have eaten sixty between the three of them. She remembers, as though it were only yesterday, watching the* panipuri *vendor's strong wrist pick up a fluffed wheat* puri, *burst the air bubble with his dirty thumb, fill it with one chickpea, a sliver of onion, one coriander leaf, then dip it into the spicy* chat *water. His hands moved fluidly from practice. Pick, burst, bury, dip. Then he put the marinated* panipuri *in their waiting palms, the water dripping down his wrist to his elbow. He had nice cityman's hands, not like theirs with the earth under their fingernails and in the creases of their palms. They had been so hungry that day at the start of their new life. It was years before that hunger would abate. Even with a full stomach, her brain would not forget those starved drought-filled days. Meha touches her flat, almost concave stomach lightly. That hunger had gone, but now it is back. Not for food. For tranquillity.*

They spent the night on the footpath, anonymous among other huddled and covered forms. Meha looked around her, unable to sleep. In the village, in their compound, she had always slept outside on hot nights, but then she knew everyone around her. In Mumbai, the noises from the street were strange, so many cars and taxis and scooters and buses. And the people were rude. She lay awake that night looking at the little strip of starless sky between two skyscrapers. There were so many people who pushed and shoved and yelled, "*Behenji,* move out of the way." *Behenji,* they had called her, *sisterji*—a term of endearment, even respect, yet it slipped glibly off tongues of people so as to barely catch in their conscience. They called her *behenji* as they pushed her. In the village, the men of other families barely looked at her, or stood aside as she passed, knowing she was not of their family. Here, already, one man had put his broad hand on her back. Bikaner whimpered, and Meha patted him back to sleep. She wondered how they would survive here in this big city.

Two seconds.

The next day Chandar started looking for work. The buildings were so big, bigger than he had seen before; he decided then that he would only work on the ground floor, near the earth that had sustained him. On the first day, he went to the Farmer's Bank because he recognized the logo. A year ago, while the sun still baked their land, his father had taken him to the local branch of the bank for a loan. Chandar could not read or

write very well but he had memorized the logo of the bank—
cutouts of two farmers, axes slung over their shoulders.

"What is it you can do?" the manager had asked him.

"Till soil, plant rice, harvest . . ." Chandar's voice had trailed
away as he looked around him. Here on the concrete floor no
soil showed, green fans clanked noisily on a whitewashed ceiling. Big, fat, leather-bound ledgers sprouted on desks. Clerks,
looking important, dug into numbers and endless cups of chai,
and unlike his field, the walls closed in on him.

"*Chalo bhai,* get out of here." The manager went back to
his office and slammed the door.

But Chandar was a persistent man. Every morning as
Meha and Bikaner fought on the street for food scraps, as
they dug through the dustbins for leftovers, he greeted the
manager at the bank, "Find me something, sahib. Any job, a
few rupees a month. I have a wife, a son."

"So do I," said the manager brusquely. At the end of the
week the security guard fell ill, and lithe, strong Chandar, his
muscles defined by years in the fields, took his job.

*Meha tries to look at her outstretched hands but they blur in front of
her eyes. She knows they are withered and old, creased at the knuckles.
But for twenty years they had served her well.*

The money still was not enough. The bank job brought in
only a few rupees, barely enough for food. One night as

they lay on the footpath looking up at a cloudy sky, Meha said to Chandar, "Geeta said her memsahib's neighbor lady needs a *bai*."

He turned to her, his voice harsh. "My wife will not be a maidservant. We are a proud people, Meha. What will the village elders think if they knew? I forbid you to go; you will not be a *bai* like Geeta."

"But Chandar, how long will we live like this? Geeta says the monsoon will come next month. There is no money to even buy a tarpaulin to shelter us."

Chandar shook his head stubbornly, refusing to meet her eyes. Meha lay beside him in silence. What pride was there in living like pariah dogs on the street? She slid an arm over his chest. A man passing on the street snickered, then stood over them watching. They stayed very still and soon he wandered away. Meha touched Chandar's face and her hand came away wet with hot tears. She laid her hand back on his chest, over his thumping heart. The next morning she went with Geeta to the neighbor lady's house.

Slowly, very slowly, the money came. Bikaner went to school. It was nothing like the village *patshala* with its drowsy, cane-wielding schoolmaster. This school was a thin building of three stories, fifty children to a classroom, and women teachers in bright saris. Uniforms and *chappals* were required and so Meha went to the bazaar near Dadar station and bought them, watching the rupees dissolve in her hand. But she understood that it was necessary for Bikaner to go to school. At home in the village, it would not have been necessary, but here even a peon was an Intermediate pass, or at least had appeared for the exams.

Meha and Chandar learned that even this last distinction—having sat for the school passing examination, though not necessarily having passed it—would sway a prospective employer. So they wore the same village clothes they had brought with them for two years so that Bikaner could go to school. In the beginning he came back very often in tears, his uniform torn from schoolyard tussles, for he fought with almost every child in his class. His spirit bent under the weight of ignorance and jibes. Why did he know so little, he asked Meha. Why hadn't they tried to teach him more? The village *patshala* schoolmaster had only taught him the alphabet, and that only in Hindi and Marathi, even though Bikaner was almost seven. Here he was taught English, the teacher recited strange-sounding nursery rhymes, Bikaner was bigger than all the children in his class (they were only four years old!)—the humiliations were endless.

Through all these cries, Meha was patient. Wait, she had said, taking Bikaner in her lap, in a year you will be in the right class. She tried to explain to him how they had had so little money for food and water these last few years, and so he had not gone to the village school regularly, and Bikaner would grow furious. When he quietened, she sat up with him every night after dinner under the orange halogen streetlamp, pointing out the letters he was to copy one by one. What is this? Z, he would laugh as he replied. You don't even know Z, Ma. Idiot Ma. But she persisted, learning the unfamiliar shapes and sounds from him and in the process teaching him.

She opens her mouth and says, "Za-ye-d." Just the way Bikaner had taught her. Pronouncing it wrong as usual, she knows. A little smile wells up in that great aching space her heart has turned into for these last four years. It was during those moments, sitting under that streetlamp, Chandar sleeping nearby in the darkness, that she had finally found something akin to affection for her son. He had laughed at her attempts to make out the curves and lines, had made fun of her, but they had learned together.

Three years passed on that footpath. They were moved a few times. Each time the good citizens of Mumbai considered the footpath-dwellers a blight on the landscape, they moved. From one footpath to another, in another street, in another part of town. In each place, there were new people to get used to, new sounds to block out at night, new bus routes for Bikaner and Chandar to learn. Then for another two years they rented a shack in a *jhopadpatti*—rows of thatched huts with a dirty canal on one side and an array of skyscrapers on the other. As she walked on the street between the huts of the *jhopadpatti,* Meha would look up at the flats towering above them and think of mosaic floors, concrete walls, a toilet that flushed, water out of taps.

All the money she saved was put into an account at the bank by her memsahib. Every night almost, Chandar and Meha would look over the passbook and she would explain the numbers to him, trying to remember what her mistress had taught her. Here was the credit column, here was Chandar's monthly salary paid in, here was the fifty rupees in the debit column they took out to pay for firecrackers for Diwali. Slowly, the credit column grew and Chandar and Meha had enough for a down payment on a tiny flat on the outskirts of Mumbai. One bedroom, a kitchen, a bathroom, a small balcony. Three hundred and fifty-six square feet with walls. It was in one of the big buildings on the sixteenth floor. For the first few months Meha walked up the stairs every day, not trusting the old, clanking lift. It terrified her to get into that iron box with its metal crisscross folding screens. The first time, she held her breath almost all the way up, watching blocks of concrete and open floor spaces rise successively before her eyes. It frightened her to live so far above the earth that she loved. She did not look down from the balcony for many years.

They adjusted to Mumbai life and became Mumbai-ites. Meha survived the big city, thrived in it in fact, and Chandar continued his job as guard at the bank. Those were happy days, with no foreshadowing of what was to come. Bikaner finished his Intermediate and even got a BA in economics and then sat for clerical exams at the Farmer's Bank.

The first day he went to work, pride in their son nearly killed both Chandar and Meha. She woke early that morning to iron his shirt, his polyester-cum-cotton-weave pants, even his undershirt. That morning as a special treat, Meha put the *chappatis* and curried eggs in front of Bikaner instead of his father.

Chandar left first in his khaki security guard's uniform, the name and logo of Farmer's Bank emblazoned across his chest pocket in red thread. Bikaner left at nine-thirty A.M., a whole hour after his father. Meha cried as she swirled the flame of the *aarti* around his bright face and marked his forehead with a streak of vermilion.

By the time Bikaner arrived at the bank, Chandar was already on his stool outside the huge glass doors. The heat had begun to pick up and beads of sweat dotted his forehead under his Nehru cap. He leapt up smartly and brought his hand to his forehead.

"*Salaam,* sahib," he said, almost choking.

Bikaner stopped and looked at his father. "Bapa . . ."

"Go, go inside, sahib," Chandar said, opening the door for him. Waves of air-conditioned air swung out and Bikaner squared his shoulders, wiped his sweaty palms against the front of his shirt and stepped into the bank. Behind him, reverently and firmly, Chandar shut the glass door.

Later he told Meha of this first morning, because she pestered him about it. When he came to this part, she had been anxious. Why are you ashamed? she remembers asking him. Not ashamed, just . . . now Bikaner is a big man. We should not pull him down, he can go far, he had said.

★ ★ ★

Meha shakes her head and closes her eyes, thinking of this man next to her, her husband of so many years. What a big mistake that had been.

No one at the bank knew Bikaner was his son. Chandar saw no reason why they should. His place was here, on the concrete steps leading to the bank—and Bikaner's was on the other side, enclosed in an English-speaking, ledger-rifling glass world where a uniform did not point out his occupation.

For the next few months, as Chandar salaamed with alacrity and jumped from his stool to open the door, Bikaner's nods of greeting became more and more distant, just like the other clerks and officers at the bank. The only time he looked at his father was when he was slow in opening the door. But Chandar did not complain. Every day, at least a few times, he flattened his face against the sunglare of the glass and looked with pride at the bent, well-oiled head of his son, the bank clerk. Every day, Chandar came home with his uniform armpits and back ringed with sweat and the soot of Mumbai, and Bikaner returned home flush with the pink coldness of air-conditioning.

Three seconds.

A year later, while Meha pored over horoscopes of girls for Bikaner, he told them he wanted to marry a fellow clerk at the bank. Chandar knew the girl, of course, but he told Meha later that night that she was of a different caste. Even after seventeen years in the city, Meha and Chandar were not used to living shoulder-by-hip with people from all castes. Things were simpler at home where they rarely met or saw other communities. Everything had an unquestioned system—the village well, the *patshala,* the vegetable market timings, but here. . . . They thought for a long time, agonizing almost. Bikaner was going to bring home a bride who was not Kshatriya, not of their warrior caste. But things were changed now, everyone said so. Besides, they could not argue with their son. He had told them of the girl, not asked their permission.

Their first shock came when she visited with her parents. Meha cleaned the flat meticulously. The mosaic floor shone with scrubbing; their mattresses and bed linen were piled neatly in one corner; the kitchen counter glowed with trays of golden *laddus* and *jalebis* and onion *bhajjias;* and ginger and cinnamon simmered in the chai water, awaiting the guests and tea leaves. Meha dressed in her second-best sari, a green-and-pink Banarasi silk Chandar bought for her the day Bikaner started working. Then they found they had no *paan* at home. Chandar rushed out to the corner shop for ten *paan* leaves and a small packet of betel nuts. On his way back, he met his future daughter-in-law and her parents.

She stopped and looked at him in surprise. "Why, Chandarnath, what are you doing here?"

He stood at the bottom of the stairs gazing at her

stupidly, a deep ache beginning to fill him. The only thing he could think of was that Bikaner had not yet told her who his parents were. His words came out with a slow, cold force. "I live here."

The smile on her face faded briefly. She patted her sleek hair and said, "I am here to see my new in-laws. Bikaner Sahib, you know."

Chandar nodded, the *paan* weighing down on his hands. There was nothing to do but follow her upstairs. They got into the lift together, Chandar standing at the very back, counting the levels with his eyes on the ground. At the sixteenth floor, he got out also. The girl said, "Did Bikaner Sahib hire you to do some extra work for today?" Then she ignored him as they all went to the door. Meha saw their confusion and threw questioning glances at Chandar, but he explained nothing, simply slipping into the flat to take his place by his son, his hands folded in a *namaste*. To her credit, the girl too covered up her shock. A wedding date was arranged.

By now, the tiny flat Chandar bought had tripled in value. It was fully paid off. In Mumbai where every little square inch was covered with either humanity, animals, hoardings or buildings, Chandar and Meha owned three hundred and fifty-six square feet of prime property. The local paper said that even in New York City space was not so expensive. The new daughter-in-law settled in quite happily in the bedroom while Meha and Chandar slept on the floor of the kitchen. The flat was more than adequate compensation for a security guard father-in-law. But the girl insisted that

Meha stop working; she could not go to the bank and tell her colleagues that her mother-in-law cleaned other peoples' latrines, she said.

When she spoke like that, Meha was ashamed too. For many years she had swept and mopped floors, washed vessels and clothes, kneaded *atta* for *chappatis,* cleaned latrines, even wiped the snotty noses and the dirty bums of her mistresses' children. The money she earned had paid in part for the flat, had paid to get them off the footpath into their own home. But now she was ashamed.

Bikaner and the daughter-in-law had two children; first, a boy born much in the same mold as his father, then a girl who looked like Meha. Then Chandar retired. The bank rewarded his loyalty with a small pension and a gold-plated watch.

Over the years Bikaner had grown more and more irritable with his parents, somehow more restless with himself. Meha wonders if they had done something wrong, if there had been some way to teach him peace along with those alphabet lessons under the halogen streetlamp. It was not something taught, but something earned, she knew. For all their troubles, Chandar and she still smiled. They smile even now. Now when there is no turning back.

Bikaner tried to pass the officer-grade exams three times; his failures reduced him to a caricature in the office. He came home every day in a bitter mood. Meha tried to console him. Better not to be an officer, *beta,* she had said, too many transfers to small towns and villages. Better to be a clerk. Bikaner shouted at her when she said anything, and Meha was reminded of those early days when he did not know English, when his schoolmates had called him names, *lallu,* lout, clod, farmer's son, as though that last were an insult. Bikaner wanted to be a manager one day. Clerks did not become managers. Officers did. Everything snapped the day Chandar retired from the bank. He had come home, his eyes full of tears, the watch gleaming on his wrist.

"Give it to me," Bikaner said all of a sudden as they were eating dinner.

"What?"

In response Bikaner leaned over, wiped Chandar's hand on a nearby towel, and slipped the watch off his hand. He said calmly, "I would be an officer if you were not a *chowkidar* at the bank. Do you think they don't know that you are my father? Why do you think I have not passed the exam? Because I am a farmer's son—worse yet, a *chowkidar*'s son."

It was as though he had hit Meha.

All this time it has been strangely peaceful, almost joyful. At this memory Meha flinches. She hopes Chandar does not see the pain in her eyes. Shiva, let him not remember that day, she prays. Not now. Not now.

★ ★ ★

"What are you doing, Bikaner?" Meha cried. "Give your father back his watch."

He ignored her and kept on eating. Chandar, stunned into silence, put a hand on his son's shoulder. *"Beta . . ."*

"Keep your hands off me!" Bikaner yelled, and even as Meha and Chandar reacted to the sound of his voice, he lifted a meaty arm and slapped Chandar's hand away.

The sound of the slap echoed through the silent flat as a red flush spread over Chandar's hand. He looked at his hand and then at his son in disbelief. His son had hit him. How could it be? How could he even raise his voice at his father, let alone . . .

An hour later Bikaner was penitent. He came to beg forgiveness, touched Chandar's feet with his forehead. He even cried as he had when he was a child, with great, heaving sobs. But the watch stayed on his wrist. It was a sign of things to come. Chandar's pension was deposited into Bikaner's account at the bank. Bikaner was briefly shamefaced, but insistent about this and they let him be, thinking that all they had was his anyway. A few days later, when Chandar sat where Bikaner did not want him to sit, the back of the son's hand slashed across the father's face. Again, he apologized, but there was more time before the apology and less sincerity in it. When Chandar stopped to talk with a friend on the street while bringing the children home from school, the broomstick was used to thrash him.

From this point on, there was only Bikaner's anger, no more justification, no explanations, no regrets. Over the next few years Meha and Chandar grew frail with fear. They talked in whispers. They were moved out of the kitchen to the balcony, huddling in one damp corner during monsoon nights. Bikaner's voice and his beatings just grew louder and wilder. The daughter-in-law stayed aloof, seeming not to see or hear anything—these were not her parents, but Bikaner's. He could do what he chose with them. It did not distress Meha and Chandar; they had not expected much from her and got little. But from Bikaner . . .

There was no room for disbelief, no one to turn to. The shame of being beaten by their own son made Chandar and Meha dumb. Although Bikaner did not beat his mother, merely pushed her around when he was angry. They did not step out of their four-by-six balcony. When they had first bought the flat, Meha had looked down from the balcony at the concrete below and shuddered. So far from the earth, so high in the sky. When she went out to hang the clothes she always did so without looking down. Now they lived on the balcony, and did not go anywhere.

But where would they go? Whose eyes could they meet anymore? The neighbors were not allowed to see their pain because they would not allow it. The neighbors all knew, of course. They had heard Bikaner's yells, heard the sounds of his beatings, perhaps even heard Meha cry. Yet Meha and Chandar could not have borne pity. That much pride still stayed in them, fierce and unrelenting. They would not turn to strangers for help. This was a family matter.

But finally it got to be too hard to stay outside on the

balcony all the time. Chandar lost weight; Meha did too, but she only saw Chandar's pain. His bones stood out brittle in his face, his shoulders bowed under the weight of a son's betrayal. Meha wrote to one of Chandar's brothers, digging deep inside herself for words to call him to Mumbai, to tell him to look after them. But before she could mail the letter—she had thought of asking the neighbor's wife for a stamp—Bikaner saw it lying underneath a bundle of their clothing in the balcony. That evening, huge ugly weals sprang on Chandar's back. A punch in the chest left him gasping with two broken ribs. Bikaner still would not touch his mother, even though Meha tried to come in the way of the beatings.

The next day—*yesterday, Meha thinks, was it only yesterday*—Bikaner came to them with a sheaf of papers. He covered the top and pointed to a line and said, "Sign here."

Chandar, propped against the balcony wall, one hand held under his ribs to support the pain each time he breathed, turned away from this monster he had created from his own flesh. "No." The word came out quietly. He would not sign what he could not read. He would not sign what they both knew to be the title to the flat to be turned over to Bikaner.

That denial cost him the hand he was holding to his chest. Bikaner pulled it away and bent the fingers back one by one until the bones broke. In her corner, Meha cowered, screaming in whispers. Bikaner turned to her and grabbed her hair in his fist. Dragging his mother to his father, he shoved her head in front of Chandar and said, "Sign, you *matachoth,* or I will throw her over the balcony."

48

When she heard that word, Meha, who had been pulling weakly at Bikaner's grip on her hair, dropped her hands over her ears. Shiva, she cried to herself, how could he call his father that? *Matachoth. Matachoth.* Motherfucker.

The fingers of his right hand hanging by his side, his chest wheezing with every breath, Chandar signed the papers with his left hand. That night, lying against each other, they made their decision.

It was too late for anything else. Too late to change what they could have done to make Bikaner a better man. When he was five, the little monkey had been smaller than him. As an adult, the bank officers' exam had defeated him, and there was nothing he could do about it. Except this, perhaps. Chander and Meha were too old, too feeble to defy him.

In some senses, Meha thought, they had steadfastly shut Bikaner from their lives. At first it was because they did not want a child, then because they did not want *him*. He had been such a flimsy child, one with so little strength of character. It had been easy to be repelled by him. Easy to turn to each other, to have Bikaner only at the fringes of their affection for each other. And Bikaner knew this. But now, all that mattered to Meha was that Chandar and she would take this last step together. To a place where Bikaner could no longer touch them, where he was not invited, where they would go without him.

She helped him, Meha thinks, she helped the man who had come to her that first night they were married and called her jaaneman. *Chandar had no more strength left, so Meha held his hand and pushed him off. Then she clambered off the ledge of the balcony she was even afraid to look down from, and launched her thin-with-hunger body into the air, down sixteen stories.*

She watches now as he hits the ground with a soft thud, blood spurting from his head, a rib protruding under his white kurta. *So long, she thinks, it takes so long to meet death. So much time since they stepped off the balcony ledge into the night. Before they left Meha wrote out their story, in her broken English, using the language Bikaner had taught her. The papers lie folded in Chandar's* kurta *pocket, now already stained with his blood. But people must know, Meha thinks, that their lives were once worth something. That they once lived and breathed and loved. That they did not ask for this end, although they made it happen. People must know. . . . There is no shame anymore about a son who beat them.*

They have fallen without a sound through the dark night, for they were always quiet people. Except for that laugh at the beginning when Meha first stepped out. That feeling had been like those early days of their marriage when they laughed all the time, when they smiled, when they were joyous.

She wants to touch Chandar again, this one last time before the end, but she knows she will land away from him. She closes her eyes as the ground comes to meet her.

The final thought is . . . how long did it take?

The Faithful Wife

*Though destitute of virtue, or pleasure seeking
else-where, or devoid of good qualities, yet
a husband must be constantly worshipped as
God by the faithful wife.*

—Manu Smriti, THE CODE OF MANU
(c. 200 BC–AD 300)

It is the letter that brings him back, because he did not know she could even write. So he comes here to stand in the courtyard, in front of this man who was once so beloved. The letter rests carefully folded in his shirt pocket, the strap of his camera holding it to his chest. The man seated in the arm-chair, his grandfather, will never see it. He has not even asked why Ram is here. Anger claws at the air around them, cleaving through their stillness. But outside, in the village that hugs the foothills of small, unnamed hills, all is still quiet.

Morning mist hangs gracefully over Pathra, swallow-ing the small village in its white folds, swirling between the leaves of the many-armed banyan in the center square. The streets leading in, rutted by bullock carts, are empty. In a few hours, the square will be noisy with life: village elders sitting in choice spots under the banyan, pedantic with endless cups of chai; women gossiping on their way to the vegetable market; urchins chasing stray dogs with a reckless wickedness that comes only in childhood.

Generations have thus used the old banyan, the village square, the vegetable market—why, even ancestors of the pariah dogs. Now, though, there is the added blare of film songs on the chai shop radio. Yet this is an outward change. Inside, in the people, the village lives in many ways like it did hundreds of years ago.

And that is why Ram is here.

On this cold December morning, as the sun struggles to burn away the mist and announces the arrival of a new day, the square is silent. A cock crows valiantly in the distance, sounding surprised at the lateness of the hour. Within the houses, wives and daughters awake to sweep doorsteps and light *chulas* that will burn well into the night. Later these women will join the throng in the market, shopping bags hung on arms strong from hard work. In the grandfather's house, however, there is no such simple peace for the two men in the inner courtyard.

The man in the chair has seen many years; his hair is whitened by the hand of time, his skin creased by sorrow, and love, and hatred through the years, each stamping its signature. The other, in normal times, is impudent with impassioned eyes and a shock of brilliant black hair. Apart in their thoughts, the younger still has the look of the older; his mother was bred of the man in the chair, and she has given to the boy the fire in his eyes, and the chin that stands firm even against his grandfather.

The old man moves finally, his hand striking a match against the grainy wood of his chair. As the match flares in the damp morning air, Ram looks up, lifting a defeated face. His hair falls in an uncombed mass over his forehead. His clothes are crumpled—the suit stained, the previously white shirt no longer a recognizable color, the tie long discarded. Mud cakes his once-shiny shoes, creeping up the cuffs of his trousers in tendrils of brown.

The journey from the city to Pathra was long. He had caught the last train in just enough time. From the station, there was the bone-jolting bus ride with a driver who sped on the hillside roads aided by a bottle of local arrack. Finally, both the old bus and its drunken driver had broken down, leaving the passengers stranded in the cold, dark, raining night. Anger was impossible—this, the passengers clucked to themselves, lifting out their baskets of mangoes, and chickens, and sleeping children, was karma after all. Ram let himself out of the bus, swung his satchel and camera over his shoulder, bent his head to the rain, and trudged the last weary kilometers to Pathra. Once there, he noiselessly came into this house.

They received him in silence; his grandmother with frightened eyes and an unsmiling face, his grandfather with a mere grunt before leading him to the courtyard. That was a half hour ago. The cup of tea at his grandfather's elbow—none was offered to Ram—has long cooled with an accusing skin of cream. Now they look at each other with the circling awareness of animals in the wild, waiting for a voice to break the silence.

Finally, the old man speaks, and out of his mouth comes the age-old vernacular of the village. This matter is too significant for the use of mere English, which both men speak fluently. "Why did you come, Ram? You should have stayed away."

All through the journey Ram has formulated questions and answers with angry words. But when he speaks, he cannot raise his voice against his grandfather, and he replies in the same language, "I could not, Nana. How can anyone stay away from what is to happen here this evening?"

His grandfather glowers. He takes a long drag from his hand-rolled *beedi* and spits out his pre-breakfast *paan* on the dirt floor of the courtyard, leaving a red streak in the mud.

Outside the house, in the main square of the village, the men are gathering with their logs of wood. This is why the letter brings Ram here. He cannot see the men, but now, with the mist still swirling around the courtyard, he hears them. Or, rather, he hears the definitive thud of one log bouncing off another as the men stack them. Somewhere along these hills lies a partially denuded forest that has given its trees so that here in Pathra a human life can be taken.

Ram shivers, wrapping arms around his thin chest, his

damp clothes clammy against his skin. His resolve is now tougher. He is here because he could not stay away, and he is here because he wants an answer from his grandfather.

Ram does nothing in small measures, loves no one in little bits and pieces, speaks his mind as the thoughts come, unedited and raw. But now he is made dumb by a hand he does not recognize. In the cold morning light he stands before a grandfather suddenly turned into a stranger. This man has held him on his knee and talked for long hours. From his words, from his voice, have grown the kings and gods adorning the walls of Hindu mythology, painted real by Nana's belief and Ram's imagination. From him has even come Ram's name. It is the name of a god exiled by his own father at the behest of a wicked stepmother. It is the name of a god who keeps his faith in that very father—why, even his stepmother—to return triumphant at the end of his exile and claim his kingdom. And thus has Nana taught Ram to believe implicitly in his elders. And that bright-eyed child, Ram, nestled against an aging shoulder, listening to the comfortable rumble in the rheumatic chest, learned to love this man, learned, or so he thought, to know this man. Today, both that knowledge and those beliefs are shaken. Ram cannot have as much faith as the god whose name he bears.

Last year when Ram came to visit Nana, he spent warm days talking with him, seated leaning against the verandah pillars, watching Nana's face glow as he recounted tales of

Ram's childhood. Today, Nana seems suddenly older, his hair whiter, the grooves on his face more pronounced; and in his eyes burns a fervor of righteousness Ram wants to wipe away.

"Your mother was too lenient with you, wretch," the grandfather grates out. "She let you have your way too often. You have to learn that one cannot always have one's way."

Ram flushes. He shifts his weight from one foot to another, wishing his grandfather will bid him sit. It will be unthinkable to do so without Nana's permission. There are some borders Ram can never cross; he has been taught too well. He fills his lungs with a deep cold breath and asks, "Do you condone what is to happen here tonight, Nana?"

As soon as he asks the question he shuts his eyes tight, willing his grandfather to give him the answer he wants, hoping yet not daring to hope for that answer. Nothing matters at this moment, not the mud caking his shoes, nor the damp misting his hair. The cold, the discomfort, have all gone away, awaiting only his Nana's response.

"It is the will of God."

Ram opens his eyes and stares at his grandfather, whose head is bent to the ground.

"God's will?" he cries, the answer tearing inside him, one border crossed already with that raised voice. "What god wills you to condemn a twelve-year-old child to her death for something she is not responsible for?"

"Enough!" the old man roars, veins standing out on his scraggly neck. "It is not your place to question a custom that has been passed on from generation to generation for over two thousand years. Who are you, with your Westernized customs and morals, living in the city with no contact with the village, to question our way of life?"

"It is against the law, Nana. You know that, the villagers know that. And why is it no one else has heard of the Sati? What are you all afraid of? If the police find out, the entire village will be arrested. By keeping quiet about it, all of you—yes, even you—are conspiring to murder a child."

Ram stops abruptly, sensing he has said too much. There is a brief moment, a brief pang when he wishes the words could be taken back, swallowed deep within himself; when he wishes he is that child on this man's knee again, trusting and trusted. But it is too late now. Tied as he is by blood and love to this man, he has to speak.

How could the Sati be right? Some customs were always wrong, however old they were, and this was something *he* had taught Ram. How could it be right for a widow to go to her husband's funeral pyre to immolate herself alive, to go with him where he went even after death? It is too bizarre even to be contemplated. This is a story from history, a past to be forgotten, not relived under the bright, harsh gaze of the twenty-first century. This is a story from his myth/history–filled *Amar Chitra Katha* comics, where women jumped off scaffolding into huge bonfires upon their husbands' deaths to avoid capture by invaders. But this is to happen here today; there are no invaders, no marauders, no claimants upon the woman's—little girl's—reputation.

Just a vicious need to connect with the past, with a willing scapegoat.

Ram shifts his weight from one foot to another. His legs ache for the release of rest but his mind will not let him do so yet. He is here in Pathra in quest of a story that fascinates him as a journalist, that horrifies him because it is going to happen with the unconscious blessing of his grandfather.

The dead man in question has died a natural death at the age of sixty-three, and less than a year ago he married the twelve-year-old daughter of a peasant. That in itself is illegal, but shrouded in the safety of an ancient village where people talk little of these things lest their way of life disappear to the will of an incomprehensible urban god, all things are made legal. Now the child, barely into puberty, barely even a woman, is to die in the fire of her husband's funeral pyre just to uphold her family's honor and their prestige. Not to mention, and this is rarely mentioned but mostly taken for granted, the few thousand rupees the old man paid for his child bride.

Ram would never have heard of this but for one incident. The village code, extending strictly even to minor things, was broken by a woman who all her life followed the rules society laid down for her in rigid lines. All her life, until now. When she opened the door for him this morning, in her eyes he had seen fear but also, in that grim glance, defiance.

The news comes to him through his grandmother, a few lines penned in the greatest hurry. It catches him by surprise. Ram has never seen her write or read. He has never heard an opinion from her unless it was delivered to a woman in the family, or to him when he was very young and so not yet a man. Nani has always followed the rules. Yet there was the childish scrawl on the scrap of paper tucked into an old envelope. The previous address on top was scratched out and topped with his own. Inside she has not asked him to come—she rarely asks for things—but has simply said, Beta, there will be a Sati here in two days, the child is only twelve, her husband, whose body lies on a block of ice in his home awaiting the cremation, is the man we talked of when you were last here.

For two hours Ram sits at his desk at the *India Times,* phones ringing on other reporters' desks around him, fans whirring on the whitewashed ceiling. Weighted sheets of paper flutter to the rhythm of the fans. The letter lay spread under his palms. Nani wants him to come, that much he knows for sure. But why? Is it the journalist she wants or the grandson?

So Ram rushes to the village, hoping the Sati will not take place and yet, in a sense, understanding that it will. As he trudges the last kilometers to Pathra in the rain, Ram knows he will never talk to the woman with gentle eyes who sent him the letter, that she will never admit to it. But as she opens the door, he sees in her spine the strength his mother has, not just from her father who shows it more obviously, but also from her mother who quietly speaks when it is time to be heard.

"This is not murder," says the grandfather, his voice

shaking with rage. He cuts into Ram's thoughts with that voice. "She chose the Sati."

"*She* chose the Sati?" Ram is incredulous. "She is twelve years old. What does she know about the Sati, or, for that matter, anything at all? She is a child, Nana. A baby. A brainwashed little child."

"You can do nothing about the Sati."

"Oh, yes, I can," Ram replies, speaking first always, thinking later. Then he stops. Could he? All through the long night, while the scenery passed by him in flashes of shadows and light, he thought hard about his decision to come to Pathra. His first instinct as a journalist had been to pick up his camera and race to the railway station. Then, running for the train, on the train, on the bus, on foot in the dark night, he had worried about his intent, his responsibility. Should he simply inform the police and let the Sati be stopped? Or should he report the incident, after the fact, in a detached manner? Somewhere, in the back of his mind, a little voice told him that this Sati could be stopped, but there would be others, in other villages. Until this one took place, until it was reported in all its horror to the country, people would not choose to condemn it. Ram knows too that the mere suggestion of a tragedy is never as powerful as the *fact* of it.

"Nana," he says, subdued, "tell me, do you condone it? If you do, when you die, would you want Nani to be put in the same situation? Would you want her to be burned alive on your pyre?"

The old man's eyes stray to the other end of the court-yard, where his wife of fifty years is pounding wheat. As the sun, struggling through the mist, sends amber fingers into the yard, chaff swirls around her in golden motes. As if sensing his gaze she looks up from her work and smiles. Both men see that smile, and in that instant, Ram realizes his grandfather knows who has brought him here. Nani has not spoken to Nana of what she has done, but he has known . . . and said nothing to her.

"The matter was decided by the village elders and the girl was told about it. To become Sati is a great honor, it is the mark of a woman's respect for her husband." The old man speaks slowly, resistance ebbing from his aged body. "It is not a decision of which I approve. I know"—he waves away Ram's unsaid words—"I am a member of the *panchayat,* but I did not vote on the matter. I suppose by my silence I assented. But what kind of a life will she have as a widow? With no money, no one to support her?"

"She will at least have a life," Ram says quietly. "That is more valuable than honor, and prestige, and reputation."

"Yes." The old man rolls another *beedi* and lights it care-fully, cupping his hands around the flame. "But a mere life is not enough . . . it is hollow, meaningless, without honor."

"You can say no, Nana."

The grandfather shakes his head. "There are things you do not understand. This child is a widow, marked with sin because of it. She can never marry again. She will have to shave her head, throw off her jewelry, cast away her glass bangles, never wear flowers. She cannot laugh out loud, or argue, or play. Her very presence is a blight to her family. She can go nowhere, be part of nothing—no weddings, no celebrations, she will be considered an ill omen."

"This is unfair. Stupid. Ridiculous. No one lives like this anymore, Nana. Does her life not have any value at all? Do her parents not love her? Do they prefer to see her die, and thus, this horrible death?" Ram knows all these rules for Hindu widows, but they are so archaic, so senseless. "Do you believe this to be her fate if she lives beyond her husband?"

And again, there is that silence, until the old man raises his gaze to his grandson's and holds it steadily. "Yes. This is her fate. She cannot change it. This is what she was born to do. If she were my child . . . I might have done differently. But I cannot, will not fight against her parents' decisions. You must accept this, Ram. There are some things we must not battle. Know this, learn from this. This child will die, so that others do not have to."

"How is this even fair, Nana?"

"What will you do about this, Ram?" his grandfather asks. "Will you rage against it? Or will you do something? Write about this. Tell the world; break the silence that hangs over this village. Do what your grandmother wants you to do." He slants his head toward the other end of the courtyard where his wife has stopped pounding the wheat and listens instead to his voice.

Ram sits down on the dirt floor, another border crossed

unbidden, and leans his back against his grandfather's chair. This is what he has wanted—to know that his grandfather is a man with a heart. And this, he realizes, is what Nani wants too. Even after fifty years she will not ask this question of her husband—she uses her grandson to do so. Ram turns his face away for a moment as his eyes fill. The pain in his chest subsides as though a familiar hand soothes it away, and then comes back again, this time for that child who waits in the village to become a martyr.

Then he turns again to look up at his grandfather and follows the older man's gaze to the woman at the other end of the courtyard. Her pestle thumps against the stone mortar gently, but beneath her strong hands the wheat crinkles and crumbles into powder. In this most important matter, she has molded them both, perhaps she has always done so, and perhaps they—husband and grandson—are who she wants them to be.

Ram turns away again. This will be a small item tucked into the second page of the newspaper, but its importance will grow as time goes by. He will have to get it to the editor as soon as possible. The nearest phone is at the village dry-goods merchant, but Ram will not go there. Instead he will walk the five kilometers to the next village, so that anyone who overhears his conversation, albeit in English, will pay small attention. Or so he hopes anyway. He will return to the city unseen. He has to. His Nana and Nani live in this village.

As the mist finally lifts and the sun bathes the courtyard

in its golden embrace, Nana's hand steals slowly to stroke Ram's head.

STOP PRESS

She walked away from the crowd to the pyre in childlike strides, her glance unwavering. All morning she had waited for this moment in patience as the men stacked logs of wood in the center of the square.

The banyan in one corner stood forlorn, its arms beckoning. But few sat under it. They crowded instead around the men, watching with a horrible fascination as the castle of wood rose, one log interlacing another in a tight embrace. The men worked in grim silence, not once lifting their heads to acknowledge the curious bystanders. All day, there was the thump of one log clutching another, building into a grotesque fortress of death for a young child. In the end it piled higher than her, higher than the tallest man in Pathra.

As night fell, a quietness descended upon the square. In an hour, the funeral would take place. But now the square was empty, the stack of logs standing alone as a symbol of what was to come. Passersby did not avert their gaze as they went into the square. The child had been condemned to her death by an entire village. There was no remorse in any face.

Finally, one by one, clad in their best clothes—maroons, pinks, greens, and blues, mocking the widow's whites—they crept into the square. Men, women, children, even babes cradled in mothers' arms, all gathered around. Faces gave away little; eyes burned with a fanatical light.

The old shopkeeper's body was brought and laid upon the pyre. Disease had ravaged him long before death came to claim its share. He had been a small man, old and decrepit. It was hard to give him such a large share in history. In this twenty-first century A.D. he took with him on his long journey a girl who was old enough to be his wife, but too young for everything else life offered.

This is the first reported incident of a Sati in almost fifty years. The child was merely twelve, but she held herself with a dignity and poise well beyond her years. There was much she did not comprehend, much she wanted to ask, but a fatality had numbed her mouth.

Clad in the white sari of widowhood, devoid of ornaments, her face pale under ebony hair, she walked to the pyre with a look of defiance. Her husband's head was placed on her lap. Her wrists were tied to the logs of wood. Only then did her brave look falter. But it was too late. Her forty-year-old stepson walked thrice around the pyre with a flaming torch before lighting the fire. As the flames licked their way greedily upward, the girl twitched and pulled at the ropes which held her.

The crowd began chanting "Sati Ma," their voices rising to a crescendo, their hands folded in prayer to the girl who would forever be revered in their village as the epitome of wifehood. The girl screamed as the fire roared toward her. It devoured her clothes, her hair; the ropes had burned through . . . She rose for a brief moment, a living inferno, then collapsed in a heap as the fire engulfed her still form.

Sati has been illegal in India since 1829. Yet more than a hundred years later, the entire village of Pathra condemned a child to her death to uphold a dubious custom. There was no regret at the end of it. As horrible as it sounds, they all wished they had done it before. But where would they have found another child willing to listen to her elders thus? Willing to give up her life because she was obedient? The Sati was conducted in the greatest of secrecy. This reporter watched hidden behind the shutters of a house in the village square.

After the fire died down and the frenetic crowd had disappeared, the girl's family went home, their heads held high, their expressions of deep pride. Today their daughter had done what no other woman had done for a long time, even in Pathra. Tomorrow, they will build a shrine for their daughter in their house. People will come from neighboring villages for a glimpse at the garland-bedecked photograph of their child, and will pay for the privilege.

The parents had already sold their daughter once to the highest bidder: the sixty-three-year-old man who married their child. Now they have sold her again.

Fire

I come to see her because my mother insists I should. She is dying, my mother says. She has but a few more days, perhaps hours. She wants to see you this last time. I don't tell my mother that I wanted to see her anyway.

Because of Kamala.

The room is at one end of the house, away from where the others live. It is an ancestral home, cavernous-looking on the outside, inside squirreled with small, limewashed rooms. Like a maze. To get from the front door to the back, there are seventeen different ways. I know. I counted them as a child. I could always escape from the caller at the front door—sometimes lodging myself under a dark, cool staircase, my frock pulled over my knees. From this vantage point the bottom half of an adult sari would pass by, bare feet flip-flopping on the mosaic floor, voice almost shrieking out my name. Payal, where are you? Be polite, Payal. Come and see your great-aunt's cousin's wife's second brother and his brood of children. Come see, and be shown.

I never went.

When she fell ill two years ago, they put her in this room away from all of them, in a part of the house I had explored a long while ago. But as I walk through the corridors and rooms, I realize that even I have never gone this far through the east wing.

There were many stories in my childhood. Of lights that came on in rooms never used. Of showerheads dripping and bathroom floors wet where no one had bathed in years. Of footprints in the untouched dust. Feet with seven toes, the maids would say. They must have had an effect on me. Even I never came this far.

Yet they have put her here. Alone. Away from all of them. As though she is an outcast, a nonentity. But I remember a time when she was powerful, when she was the only real presence in this house. The matriarch of us all, the voice that commanded, with a gaze that made my mother shrivel, that made my father grovel. How small the mighty have become.

Each day a maid trudges to her room with food, turns her over in the bed, washes down her tired limbs with tepid water, and then leaves. Each day someone in the family visits her. They take turns, my mother says. Draw lots. She never talks to them. She knows that they all blame her now.

For what she did to Kamala.

My feet slow and drag as memories come back.

Of gentle, quiet Kamala. Yet with a smothered fire inside her that on two—no, three—occasions, burned fervent. I bore witness to two of them. It is because of the third I am here. Because of what she did to Kamala. Because what they all—the people in this house—did to Kamala.

Fire.

In my childhood, we were twenty-one people in the house. My mother and father, of course, and aunts and uncles who were not terribly good at having or keeping jobs, and their even more useless children. And the servants.

The fat cook, who amply sampled every dish before it got to us. Just tasting, Amma, he would say. The *mali* whose thumb had never been green, who let the grass grow wild, yet who could coax rare blue-purple roses to bloom against the side wall. (The neighbor would pick them slyly for her *puja,* leading to loud, choleric fights between her and the *mali.*) A man to polish my father's shoes—that's all he did, polish my father's shoes. The chauffeur, leaning against the car (he wouldn't let us lean against it) smoking his smelly *beedis* all day. The khaki-clad *chowkidar* at the front gate with hot eyes that looked at us greedily when we hit puberty. Then there were the three maids who lived in a shack in the back garden, who swept and wiped the house each day, and spent the rest of the time on the steps, their voices delicious with gossip. They seemed to disappear a lot, one after another, leaving with heavy stomachs, made pregnant by the *mali* or the *chowkidar,* or even once, the chauffeur. The men stayed. The maids left.

It was, this queen of our house had said, their fault. A woman must always know when to keep her legs closed.

The room is dark when I enter. There are windows on two walls with iron grills on them shaped like peacocks in flight. The glass panes are shut and some industrious spider has spun fanciful webs over the peacocks, capturing them in needle-thin nets. The room has not been painted in many years; the walls are chipped, some places showing a light pistachio green, some an antacid pink. Like all the other rooms in this house, it is small. The floor gleams, although the mosaic, brilliant chips dulled to blackness, has not been properly scrubbed for a long time. Perhaps not since the house was built a hundred and fifty years ago. But then, I don't think this room has been used in a hundred and fifty years.

She lies in the center of the room on a small cot. A ceiling fan clanks directly over her, shuddering with every revolution. I look at it, wondering if it will fall on her. Wishing it would.

She is on her side, barely making a dent in the mattress. A strange yet familiar old-person smell rises over her, even though I know she is clean. She has always been clean, scouring her skin with a fanatic's fervor, as though all her sins would slough away with the scrubbing. Her hair shines silver on the spotless pillow. The strands are sparse; I can see her skull through them. Everything is white around her: the sheet that covers her body; her blouse, through which gaunt arms protrude like sticks; the pearls she always wore; and her sari, of course. White, pure, spotless. To show she is a widow. To show she is faithful to her husband's memory, to show that she does not consider it worth her while to preen in gold and colored silks for another man. To show that since he died she keeps her legs closed.

I approach and draw back almost at once. Everything is white, but her skin, that creamy, rich, rose-tinted Brahmin skin, that heralder of high birth, is now a blistered ebony. As though someone stripped her of her white clothes and dipped her into a fire. Not enough to burn, but enough to scorch.

Fire.

Her eyes open as I come near again. Even her pupils are white, clouded by cataract, milky white strands over once flashing eyes. But she knows I am here. She puts out her hand, and I take it.

It is a small hand, bony, the knuckles dried with age. The veins on the back are thick green lines, like rivers frozen under her skin.

Payal. Her voice is thin, reedy, like much of her body. Payal, look at my skin now. Look at the color of it.

I am still standing looking down at her. There is no chair in the room, and I will not sit on the floor so *she* can look down at me. But after so many years of not seeing me, so many years when she must have thought about me, wondered where I was and how I was doing, she talks of her skin.

Laughter bubbles inside me, forcing its way through the lump in my throat. Look at the color of my skin, she says.

So I look. And I see the dark withered brown of chocolate gone bad. I see flecks of skin peeling from her arms. Deep lines furrow her thin face. I see her lips, dry and drawn over teeth that did not stand the test of time. These are her sins. She now wears them for everyone to see. They have come up from inside her, where she has hidden them for years. She has gone bad from the inside.

But the expression in her near-opaque eyes has not changed. And from that comes a brief memory of a time long past when she was still young. From when I can remember she has worn this white. So I did not know him, the man she had married. But her pale skin always glowed, gold with sandalwood and turmeric, tinted pink on her cheeks with a dusting of the vermilion she would wear in the part of her hair. This last, defying the color ban on widows. Vermilion was a sign of marriage, married women wore it in their hair, but she, clad in white, ears bare of diamonds, fingers ringless and slender, wore vermilion in her hair and pearls around her neck.

Only she knew where to find me when I escaped from all of them. Under the staircase, behind an *almirah,* inside an *almirah*—the smell of mothballs and neem leaves swirling among the neatly folded silk saris—or hidden in a corner of the many balconies. Payal, her voice would ring loud and strong through this house of many rooms. Payal, come down from the champa tree. Girls do not climb trees.

I always listened to her. Then she would clap her hands and one of the not-yet-pregnant maids would materialize with a plate of sweets. In many colors. Purple-tinted coconut *burfis,* flakes sprinkling the tray; slow-simmered chickpea flour *mysore pak,* a rich brown and drowning in ghee; *gulab jamuns* the color of rust, oozing cardamom-scented sugar syrup; silver-foiled cashew squares, taut from the fridge yet melting on contact with my tongue; semolina flour *laddus* rolled into balls, their uneven curves carrying the imprint of the cook's fingers.

She rewarded me with those sweets when she called for me. That was why I always came. Now looking at that brown hand in mine, I taste the sweet-sour curd flavor of *mishti dohi* in my mouth. These fingers, blackened by hatred, had once dipped into a bowl of *mishti dohi* and fed me.

We had a bond, this woman and I, even though we were years apart in age. She seemed to know what I was thinking, why I was thinking. She seemed to know what I wanted. And then after Kamala was born, she no longer knew who I was. It was as simple as that.

Why so long to come, Payal?

I meet her eyes.

How can you even ask, bitch? I speak in English, a language she is not comfortable with, but I know she understands. I will not give her the pleasure of speaking in Tamil, even though what I have to say will be so much more effective, so much more terrible in that tongue. I use antiseptic English.

Kamala. Her voice is soft; I have to lean over to hear it.

Yes, Kamala. Because of Kamala. You know it is because of Kamala.

In this house of many people, someone or the other was always having children. There was always a baby crawling around, bottom bare, peeing where it wanted, wallowing happily in that pee. And a maid mopping up when she could, or when my mother yelled at her. I never really noticed the babies, except as pesky, snot-nosed, bawling-mouthed, teary-eyed creatures. Or I should say, I pretended very hard not to notice them in case some auntie found my interest charming and left her precious little god with me while she went off shopping.

So I was an unencumbered ten years old when Kamala was born. To my mother.

It was during the summer holidays and the house seemed full of people, hiding in cool, dark corners from the heat. All of *my* hiding places. I spent that whole vacation in the champa trees, watching the squirrels protest at my presence, watching a bright snake nestle in the branches, drawn by the sweet smell of the flowers. And then Kamala was born. Small, squishy, indeterminate features. A mouth that rarely cried.

That intrigued me. How could a child possibly be so silent? But I still stayed on the periphery, skirting around her, watching from afar. Until my mother forced me to go see her properly (it is only polite, Payal, she's your sister). I think my mother had forgotten I existed for a while; she had had a difficult pregnancy, and then after Kamala came, she was busy with the visitors.

Kamala lay on a sheet on the floor following me around the room with her brilliant eyes. I think she actually smiled when I slid the gold bangles (that my mother gave me for her—a gesture of protection from an older sister) onto her tiny arms. When the holidays ended and I came home daily from school, I went to her, and she looked for me. I would lie beside her on the floor, and Kamala would grab my hair with her hands and put it in her mouth. Or she would try to entertain me by kicking her legs in the air, silver anklets trilling with each movement, the sound always seeming to take her by surprise. It was her quietness that pervaded my world. Her contentment when I held her—some auntie screaming I was to put a hand under her head for it had not set yet—her first smile, and that not for gas.

Kamala, she says again.

Her free hand, the one I am not holding, rises to touch her hair. And I know what she wants to say.

Kamala of the doe eyes, large, liquid, edged with a sweeping fan of eyelashes. We all grew up modern. Western. The aunties cut our hair short, bangs in the front, a straight sweep just above the shoulders in the back, but Kamala, dreamy, tranquil Kamala would not let them touch her head. When she was three, that inner fire burst into flames and she said no. The word frightened the whole house immeasurably, for she had not spoken yet. Not one single word. They thought, we all thought, she was mute.

She told me later she felt there had been no necessity to speak, for everything in her life so far had progressed as she had wanted it. No ripples, no waves. But when some auntie came to her with the scissors, Kamala said no. Just once. There were no arguments, no cajoling, no scolding, nothing. Just that simple no.

I did all the yelling and screaming on her behalf. I kept her behind me, away from the scissors. I hauled her up the champa tree when someone came calling with the barber my father used every second Sunday. I distracted the adults (they were easily distracted) by sprinkling sugar on the back verandah to beckon an army of red ants. It took them five days to get rid of the ants. Kamala just watched me, did not even say thank-you, for things were progressing as she wanted them. But one night, a few months later, as I was up late studying for a history exam, she came to the door of my room and just stood there. I looked at her in silence, knowing she wanted to say something, silent because she had taught me the value of it. Then she came in, reached up from the floor, put her little arms around me and laid her cheek against mine. We did not kiss much in this house; neither of us would have known how to do so. But that one embrace was enough. It was never repeated again. It did not have to be. For I knew.

So Kamala's hair grew long and luxuriant. A gleaming ebony, catching multicolored highlights in the sun. Her hair seemed almost too big and too heavy for such a small face, a slender neck, a tiny child.

I envied that hair, the old woman says now, cleaving through my thoughts. Envied its length, its brilliance, envied as she bent over her books, her hair weighing down her neck. Envied that skin. Envied her silence. No one who was so silent was normal. She cannot have been normal. Look what she did later on.

My grip tightens on her hand. I see distress darken her eyes. Bitch. Bitch. Bitch. Bitch. She does not cry out. Does not ask for help as I squeeze her fingers, my knuckles crushed against hers.

Once I loved this woman. So much. She is my grand-mother after all, my father's mother. My mother and father were always at the edges of my affection. But she consumed my hours until Kamala came. There were boys in the house—born to continue the male line, to deposit genes, to carry the name. But she ignored them and favored me. Only a girl child. I slept in her bed until I wanted a room of my own.

She taught me nursery rhymes in English, stumbling over the words. Laughing at her mistakes. With a freedom she never showed to anyone else, not even to my father, who was her only son. She told me the pearls she wore would one day be mine. After. But there was no after in her thoughts, for she would never leave me. Once she was kind and gentle. If only to me.

When the extended family came to visit, to pay their respects, I would sit by her side. Watching as she was falsely gracious. And obstinate if they wanted something (usually money) she would not give. And hurtfully sarcastic. When they left, she talked of these people who made claims on her, who thought they had claims on her. And she would smile. As though anyone but I could claim her.

Suddenly she asks, how is America?

You care how?

I always cared, Payal. Always wanted to know. It was hard, sending away one of ours to a foreign land. But you insisted, yelled to get your way, left us here alone. Went away alone. As though we meant nothing. As though you did not spend your childhood here, as though we were not family. Now it has been ten years.

Ours. Our. We. She means mine, my, I. There has never been a plural in her vocabulary, unless it included me. Stifled me. A long time ago, I had let her do this, free within her grasp, unfettered by her obsession. Until Kamala.

I was determined not to cry when I came here. But at her words, tears fill and blur my vision. I was sure I would never see this woman again all my life. Yet here I am, in this house, in this room, standing next to her. Outside the frosted windows of the room, the sun is setting now, golds and amber through insect-ridden glass. I put down her hand to go to the light switch.

She whimpers. Don't go. Don't leave me here alone, Payal.

The naked lightbulb sheds a harsh light over us. Suddenly, she is even smaller than she was when I came into the room. Her eyes move wildly, seeking me.

I bend over her again, my voice brittle and broken. Did Kamala ask for me? Did she?

Yes.

It is a small word, like the no Kamala said when they wanted to cut her hair. Yet filled with meaning. My tranquil Kamala asked for me, and I was not there. I sit down next to her, heavily, as though my bones are now as old as hers. I put my face in my hands.

Don't, she says. Don't cry, Payala.

Don't call me that!

I am angry. But mostly with myself. Angry because I was selfish enough to leave when I was twenty-one for graduate school in America. Angry because I could not stay in this house anymore with its heavy secrets, with its quarreling women, with its squirrel rooms. Angry because I left, not thinking I was leaving Kamala behind in their hands. Kamala who never spoke unless it was necessary, who let things happen around her because I was there to fight instead, who in the end, did not know *how* to fight. Whose burnished hair shone like fire in the sunlight.

Fire.

Kamala brought a puppy home one day from school. I remember the dog squealing in her arms, licking her face until saliva dripped. I remember seeing her smile. A slow, content smile, like the one when she was a baby and I held her in my arms. The smile she had given only me. The clan gathered around to look at the puppy. Kamala stood in front of them, small and slight, hair in a thick braid to her knees, the dog sitting quiet at her feet.

No, this woman said. Dogs are unclean.

Still Kamala stood in front of them, her eyes watchful, moving from one face to another. But *she* had spoken. This woman, who lies on the bed in front of me, sat in an old carved armchair. Envious of Kamala's hair. I knew what she was thinking. Good girls keep their legs closed, good girls listen when told something by adults.

I jumped in, of course. Let her keep the dog. It's only a dog. Let her keep it.

Then she slapped me. She got up from her chair, came to where I was sitting, lifted me up by my arms, stood me in front of her. And slapped me. Enough, she said. Enough of this nonsense. Kamala will not allow her hair to be cut, she said no to it seven years ago. She will not have this dog.

I was made silent by that slap. She had never even raised her voice to me before. When my mother scolded me, she yelled at my mother. No one in the house was allowed to reprimand me. No one was allowed to ask where I was, or whether I had done my homework, or studied for an exam, or come home from school on time. No one was simply allowed to do *anything* to me. Even she did not question me. Now she had slapped me and for once, I was dumb, unable to meet Kamala's eyes.

Kamala must have been ten; I was twenty. One year from going to America. One year from leaving Kamala to these people.

But even if I was losing the strength to fight, Kamala's was only just beginning. She kept the dog. Fed it scraps from the kitchen, literally taking food out of the cook's mouth. I think he even lost weight during those two months. It did not last very long.

One day, the puppy floated in the well in the back garden, his stomach distended, his eyes bulging, his tongue hanging out.

I had never seen Kamala cry before. She did then, leaning over the edge of the well, looking down into the water, her arms outstretched as though to touch the dog. She cried soundlessly, her mouth open. I did not know how to comfort her; I did not put my arms around her, or lay my face against hers, did not tell her everything was going to be all right. Did not tell her I saw this woman do it. Did not tell Kamala she had stood over the well for two hours watching the puppy swim in slower and slower circles, until exhausted, it drowned.

I just left for America.

I look up at the woman on the bed. She seems to be sleeping, her eyes are closed.

Aziz, I say.

The word fills the room. She opens her almost-sightless eyes and I see hatred burn inside them.

Do not say that name. Do not take that name in your mouth.

She turns away from me.

I force her head back to mine, force her eyes to mine.

Aziz. Aziz. Aziz. Aziz. Say it, bitch. Say Aziz. Say his name. Say Aziz.

I had spent seven years in America without coming back here. After graduate school, I got a job editing a newspaper in New Jersey. I partied at night, downing mai tais with a vengeance. I opened my legs for a few men; the American men were always kinder than the Indian men afterward when we broke up. For I always broke up. I did not care enough to be a good girl.

In seven years, only one letter came from Kamala. She sent a photo with it.

She was in high school then, twelfth grade, I think. The picture sits on my desk at home. At America home, not here home. Someone had caught her in half-profile. Her hair tumbles down her back still, and still to her knees, thick, glorious, blue-tinted like a starlit sky. Her eyes are the same, laughing even as her mouth does not. The neck still slender. The open blouse of her sari showing bones against delicate skin. Pale Brahmin skin, the skin she got from this woman. She looks at the person taking the photograph with a glance filled with love. With trust. With respect. That was why she sent me the picture, for she knew how she feels in it is how she feels for me.

Aziz took that picture with Kamala's camera.

The old woman's voice comes to me again. Brittle as mine, still filled with hatred. He was a Muslim. They eat cows; they eat the sacred Hindu cow. The Nandi. How could Kamala even bear to be near him, to touch him? It was wrong.

I eat cows, I say. In America I have eaten many many cows. American cows are not that different from Indian cows. I eat cows. Steaks, hamburgers. They mince the meat, season it with salt and pepper, slap it on a grill. The fat bubbles in the meat, sizzling over the side. Then I cut into it with a fork and a knife. I put a piece in my mouth and chew slowly, letting the juices from the meat fill my tongue. It slides down my Brahmin throat, into my Brahmin stomach. Look. I pull her hand into mine again. I rub my hand against hers. Look, you touch the skin of a woman who eats meat cooked over an open fire.

Fire.

Her head flaps against the pillow, her eyes moving sightlessly around the room. Don't say these things. Don't say you have eaten meat. Now your blood is polluted. Oh, Payala.

Don't call me that, I scream. You bitch. You horrible stupid bitch. What was wrong with Aziz after all?

He was a Muslim. The words come slowly, stubbornly. Kamala wanted to marry him, to have his children. To mix the blood of our house with his, it would not have been right. She said no when we wanted to cut her hair.

He is beautiful, Kamala had written. And she said more, painting his face for me with her phrases. A shock of curly hair, unruly over his forehead. Eyes that laughed, a mouth that did even more so. Though she did not tell me, I know he put his arms around her. I know he kissed her, his lips meeting hers in homage almost. As though he knew she had not been kissed very much in her life. I know his father owns the chai shop on the corner of the street from this house. Aziz sat there behind the counter, the steam curling his hair, his *kurta* white and pressed, starch holding it stiff even against the heat. Kamala lost her hairpin in front of the shop on her way back from school one day. He helped her look for it, scrambling in the dust of the street, his fingers brown with mud when they emerged with the pin.

Here. Then he put his hand out involuntarily, skimming over her hair, loose around her face in wisps this late in the day. You have beautiful hair. The most beautiful hair I have seen.

She knew, Kamala knew it would be Aziz. She never hid anything from the people at the house. Met him openly. Talked with him outside the shop where anyone passing could see her, always standing away from him. It was six months before he touched her hair. Six months when this woman on the bed raved, ranted, screamed herself hoarse. She locked Kamala in her room. Kamala picked the lock and walked out. She took Kamala out of school. She yelled curses at her. Kamala listened to everything, her eyes huge, silent as usual. Because she still did not think it was necessary to speak.

It was not right, the old woman says again. Not right. Not right. Not right.

I hit her. My hand comes away shaking, my fingers leave their mark on her dark face. Look at your skin now. I hold her hand up to her eyes. Look at your skin. It is because of what you did to Kamala.

No. That was right. That had to be right, she says.

Kamala ran away with Aziz one night. She had written to me about him, sent me her picture but not his. Then waited six months. I read it and remembered. How this was the first time she had written me in seven years. How she never came to the phone when I called from America. How she had been silent. I felt betrayed. I did not see then what I see now. I should have come back to India. To this house, to the child whom I thought of as my own. To my little sister, born ten years after I was born, who swept me away into her quiet world. Whom I left.

The story came to me through many people. The phone never seemed to stop ringing those first three months afterward. I would pick up the phone dreading a well-known voice from my past, yet wanting desperately to hear what they had to say. The ten thousand miles between America and India melted away as they spoke, words tumbling out of their mouths, in a hurry to point fingers, to ease the burden of their own shame. The neighbor who watched and did nothing, my aunties who participated and so did nothing, my mother who cannot speak anymore without blame coloring her voice, my father who cannot meet my eyes. Only she, this woman on the bed, never talked to me about it.

Yet they are all equally guilty.

It was less than forty-eight hours before they found Kamala and Aziz at the railway station. They were in a train, in a second-class compartment. Aziz seated near the window. Kamala leaning against him, her head on his shoulder.

They dragged them home. Dragged them from the train. Aziz resisted, but neither of them cried out. They were both quiet people.

Brought them into the front garden. Tied them to the champa trees. Stoned them.

You threw the first stone. My voice is tired now. I am tired. I feel old. It is from a pain that will never wash away. Just as the blood will not wash away from this woman's hands.

I had to, she says. I had to show everyone what was right. I had to tell them. Aziz's blood could not mix with the blood of this house. Not with the blood of a daughter of this house. They had been missing for forty-eight hours. Who knows what they had done, and where they had done it? No good Brahmin boy would ever marry her. Or marry a daughter of the house if we had not done what we did. It was right.

She hides behind a strange and immovable logic. That the family's reputation must be saved at all costs. Even if it means losing Kamala. It is true, what she says. Had they not done what they did, no decent family would marry into ours. They are all blinded by this logic, following it faithfully as though we live three, four hundred years ago. Yet this bothers all of them. Which was why various people called me in America to explain. Which is why they put this woman away.

It was the right thing to do, Payala, she says again.

Payala. She calls me Payala. As Kamala did all her life. At first, it was because her mouth could not stop at a consonant as a child. She needed to make my name musical, to add that "aa" at the end of it. Paa-yaa-laa. Later it was a joke between us. And we joked so little, I let her call me Payala.

Don't call me that, I say again. But my voice is drained of energy.

She threw the first stone. A small rock really. It cut into Kamala's chest, at the collarbone, smashing it. Kamala bled. Yet she did not cry. Then they all threw stones. My mother, my father, my aunties, the chauffeur, the maids. I know it need not have happened, I know this woman on the bed could have stopped it. The people of this house had always listened to her; if she had wanted to, she could have stopped it.

When Kamala and Aziz hung from the ropes that tied them to the tree, still silent, this woman walked up to my sister and pulled her head up by her hair. Kamala watched as she brandished a pair of scissors in front of her eyes. Holding Kamala's braid with one hand, she cut through the thick fabric of hair.

Only then did Kamala scream. Great big screams came tearing out of her. For the puppy who died in the well. For Aziz to whom she had given all her love when I left. For the children they would never have. For me.

For me who left her and went away because I could not bear to stay. For me who did not answer her letter, who did not come because I couldn't recognize a plea for help. For me who had always sheltered her when she was young. And in doing so, did not teach her how to shelter herself.

Her hair lay spread on the ground like a fan. That was when—Kamala still screaming, Aziz quiet by her side, his ribs cracked, his cheekbones smashed—my grandmother set fire to them.

Fire.

The champa trees, alive as they were, burned very well. Everyone waited in the front garden as Kamala and Aziz burned. All of them, following this woman like sheep. And she stood there watching, a stone still clasped in one hand, the scissors in another. When the ropes had burned through, Kamala lifted her hand to Aziz, to hold his. Her hair was already aflame by then, in a glowing halo around her face. She did not lift her hand to dust off the flames. She lifted her hand to join with his. When the fire died down, they found them collapsed at the foot of the charred champa trees, their hands melded in the heat, unable to part them.

Aziz's father buried them together. I know the whole neighborhood saw the fire, felt the heat, smelled the burning flesh. When the police came the next day, they found only two blackened stumps of trees. An accident, everyone said. And no one saw how it started. This is how it was, how it has always been. For we, our family, this woman, have money, and silence is cheap.

That was three years ago. Three years before I could come back. Three years and thousands of mai tais.

Did I do right? Her voice is piteous now. Look at my skin, she says. It is as black as Kamala's when she burned. Did I do right, Payala?

My mother told me to come and see her, so I do. In this house, her house really, she is the head. Even my father, who pretends to be a man, who pretends to play the role of the head of the house, is nothing compared to this woman who gave birth to him. I have seen her power, known it, broken away from it, even. If she wanted, she could have saved Kamala.

No, I say. It was not right, what you did.

She turns away from me to look toward the darkness beyond the windows. Her voice, when it comes after a long silence, is distant. You loved Kamala more.

I was thinking I should leave when those words fill the room. Suddenly, all the dull ache I carry within me focuses into pinpoints of pain. Like clear ice shards.

Is that why—?

Then I stop, the words sticking in my throat. I remember wondering why during all those nights when I was forced to think. When, my tongue still sweet-sour from a mai tai, my brain benumbed and disobedient from the alcohol, I wondered why. Now I know why. Because she thought I gave my love—the love she had to have—to Kamala.

Such a simple, stupid, stupid reason. And such simple, stupid, stupid reasoning. Did she think Kamala's not being alive anymore would make me love her again?

I look at her, black skin against white sheets. Her sins

have come up from inside her. I raise myself on my knees. My hands tremble. But I know why I have come back after so many years, and why I will never come back here again.

Look at me.

She looks.

Look at my hands. My nice white Brahmin hands. So unlike yours. Watch them as they come nearer.

I need only one hand to cover her mouth and her nose. With the other I smooth the silver hair from her forehead so I can look into her eyes. She does not even struggle. She is even defiant. Her breathing grows shallow.

No, I think. Let her live. I do not stop from fear, for if she dies, no one will condemn me. They all want her dead; for alive she reminds them of their failings. I want her to live like this, alone, unwanted, a shameful reminder. When I take my hand from her mouth and nose a deluge of fear floods through those blurred eyes. She wants me to do this. And she knows why I don't.

I turn and leave, from this house, from this city. I will never return.

I will always wonder. If I had not taken my time, myself, away from my grandmother, Kamala would be here today. Except I was imprisoned by her strange love, fighting to be free. When Kamala came, I stepped away. And in doing so, saw my grandmother clearly. In doing so, I caused Kamala's death.

But I leave with a lightened heart, her terror following

me. When at this last moment I see fear in my grandmother, I am almost happy.

For this is how Kamala must have felt when this woman cut off her hair. Not when she stoned her. Not when she set fire to her.

When she cut off her hair.

The Most Unwanted

Heat simmers thick in the air, although the sun set three hours ago, flatlining into the horizon with the *chut-phut* briskness of the tropics. One moment there was a smear of darkness, at the other a sudden deluge of it, revealing pale stars in the sky.

Nathan walks to the verandah outside his quarters and squats on his haunches on the third step leading down, his hips moving smoothly into position as his thighs fold onto his shins. A *beedi* smolders between the fingers of his right hand. In a few minutes, he can feel the inky humidity of a Chennai night run sweat lines in the curve of his bare spine, pool damply into the waist of his white *veshti*. Somewhere, well beyond the patch of trees that line this engineering school campus, the horns of auto rickshaws, buses, and scooters howl on the road, accompanied by the crash of brakes and the shout of curses.

The light is switched off on the verandah to keep away insects. Nathan puts the *beedi* to his mouth, pinching the unlit end between a nicotine-stained thumb and forefinger. He drags a mouthful of smoke. It swirls around in his mouth, rushes to fill his lungs, spews out of his nostrils. When he lowers his hand, a mosquito alights on his forearm, searching to plunge among the sparse hair. He lets it prod at him, settle to drink from his skin, and then, deliberately, lifts his other hand and smashes it into a mess of blood.

Nathan sits alone outside his quarters, a one-storied armylike barrack, low and long, whitewashed after every five monsoons. Inside, he hears the soft hiss of the gas stove, the pop and spit of mustard seeds and curry leaves in hot oil, the sizzle as his wife seasons the *rasam*. The cooking rice wafts its starchy aroma over him. He brushes his face, and massages the back of his neck with a callused hand, easing the pain that lingers there. All the while he listens for the sound of the child, his ears bending back toward his rooms.

Krishna Shiva-Rama-Lakshman.

Named for every conceivable deity in the pantheon of Hindu gods. Blue-skinned Krishna, player of the flute, herder of cows, beloved of the Gopika maidens. Shiva, destroyer of evil, mendicant in the Himalayas, possessor of the wrecking third eye on his forehead. Rama, sent to exile by a wicked stepmother, who later, irresponsibly, sent his wife into exile. Lakshman, not a god, but brother of Rama and hence by association accorded that status. Who drew a simple line in the sand so potent, a demon could not cross it to abduct his brother's wife.

And so Parvati has named her child—Nathan's grandchild.

He listens again for the child. But the boy is quiet. Asleep already, perhaps? He had eaten buffalo milk and rice for his night meal, flitting around their two rooms and tiny verandah on his little sturdy feet, Parvati in pursuit. She had laughed in delight as she followed him with the stainless steel cup, pouncing on him, filling his unsuspecting open mouth with rice and sugar milk. "Eat, Krishna *kanna.*" Eat, apple-of-my-eye Krishna.

The brown cotton string that holds the rolled-up tobacco leaf wisps into bits of smoke as the *beedi* burns low to the tips of Nathan's fingers. With one hand, he shakes out another *beedi* from the packet and lights it with the frittering end of this one.

He rubs his head. His hair is short, cropped close to his lean skull, scattered with gray. Each morning little stubbles of white decorate his chin before the razor whisks his face clean. His frame is small; Nathan has never been a big man. He will be sixty soon, and yet, his muscles flex tightly against his bones, lean from walking and riding a bicycle in his peon work. The sun has darkened his skin to so rich a mahogany that even his black eyelashes are swallowed by his face. If he smiles, two lines run alongside his mouth, deepening as the years pass.

Ever since Krishna's birth, Nathan does not smile very much.

Krishna, his daughter Parvati calls this child. Unashamed, unrepentant, unembarrassed about giving him the name. There is a story Nathan now remembers about the baby-god Krishna who would steal butter from his mother's churn. One day she chases him around the courtyard, accusing. He laughs, saying no I did not. Open your mouth, she says. Open your mouth so I can see for myself. Still laughing, the child opens his mouth. And there the mother sees— not traces of pilfered butter, but an image of the world. She draws back in wonder, in awe. Knowing this child of hers is no ordinary child, but an incarnation of Lord Vishnu come down to earth. At the time she does not even know that Krishna was not born of her, since he was brought to her bed and switched with her daughter as she slept, exhausted after childbirth. This was because he was unwanted too, by his evil uncle Kamsa who had wanted to kill him. And so the baby Krishna, born to one woman, brought up unknowingly by another, survived. The gods had wanted him to live, to grow, to battle his wicked uncle.

When Nathan remembers this story about the baby Krishna, confused and angered as he seems to be almost every day now, his memories halt at that sentence—the baby Krishna was unwanted too . . . and yet he survived, just like Nathan's grandchild.

There is the slap of naked feet on the floor of the veran-dah. Nathan shifts his head slightly on a stiff neck, watch-ing the movement out of the corner of his eye, without seeming to do so. Swamy, the watchman, comes out of his quarters and settles into a wooden easy chair sitting on the beaten earth outside. He belches loudly, patting his stomach. He yells for his wife to bring *vetalaipaak*. A few minutes later she comes out with a steel plate bearing betel nuts and leaves, sits on the dirt next to Swamy, and folds the nuts into the leaves, secures it with a clove. Nathan does not look at Swamy; he keeps his gaze away from him and straight toward the tamarind tree in the yard, now noisy with night crickets.

Around Nathan, light spills in yellow rectangles from the verandah windows, from all the others' quarters. Swamy, the watchman at the campus gates, puffed with importance at being able to deny entrance to whom he chooses. Vikram, the sweeper, who swirls his broom over the department offices, leaving brown dust under chairs and tables. Muthu, the gardener, who digs assiduously in the dry mud where nothing grows. Prashanth, the chai man—all he does is bring chai and coffee for the professors, making umpteen trips to the shop outside the campus and returning with a tray of clay cups balanced precariously on the back of his bicycle. Of course, this is a big campus, the biggest in the city, so there are other quarters for other department servants. But these quarters, attached to the Department of Electrical Engineering, are where Nathan has spent thirty-five years. In two rooms.

And here, last year, Parvati brought the child Krishna. She did not ask Nathan or his wife permission for the name; they would not have given it anyway. Preferring to let the child be nameless, for giving him a name would mean putting a name to their shame.

Swamy, the watchman, calls out to him. "Nathan sir, how are you? And your wife?"

Swamy calls him sir because Nathan is not just the eldest of those who occupy these quarters, but, by profession, the highest rank. A peon does not soil himself with menial tasks. In Nathan's barracks, he has precedence. This is something he has worked toward for many years, starting at the campus as a sweeper, then a chai man, then a watchman, and now finally, a peon.

Now Nathan nods briefly in Swamy's direction. Two years ago, before the child became public knowledge, he had status. Now these salutations are empty, meaningless—there is no real respect behind them, as though there is no more reason for Nathan to be able to hold his head high again with pride.

Swamy's wife is all smiles, her eyes aglitter with malice in the darkness. Even with his back to them, Nathan knows this; it is as though her gaze lights up the darkened yard. He hears the rustle of her cotton sari as she nudges her husband with a thick elbow. Swamy grunts heavily, clears his throat, and asks, "And your third daughter? And the child? Everything is well in your house?"

Nathan ignores him and looks at the tamarind, its fruit hanging heavy, brown with ripeness, and too high in the branches. When Parvati was a child she used to throw stones and rocks at the fruit to dislodge it from the tree and when it fell, she would gorge herself, carefully keeping the seeds. For the children of the barracks, the black smooth seeds, the size of peas, were currency. With them they traded for marbles, pieces of chalk, a broken slate, a rubber ball, flat stones for playing *pittu,* a ribbon for their hair.

The dull ache Nathan has carried around flares into a bitter pain in his chest when he hears Swamy's wife stifle a giggle. Even now, after three years, he has not learned to disregard what others say. Every effort has gone into making his face smooth and expressionless, of listening with reverence to what his betters have told him about Parvati and the child, of seeming not to care when his lessers like Swamy have slyly taunted him. But the ache does not go away.

He remembers in the dark of the night when Parvati herself was born, their third girl child.

His wife had gone for her confinement to her mother's house in the village as usual and Nathan waited for the news. The postman who brought the yellow postcard to Nathan slapped it down in front of him with a "Here. For you." Then he turned his back and went around the department giving the professors their mail.

The previous Diwali, the postman had come to Nathan for his festival *baksheesh* for the first time. Nathan had not given him any, incredulous that a postman would ask a peon, when he had not begged even of the secretaries and typists. For this Nathan was made to wait, postcard in hand, the blue ink smudged with tan fingerprints, some of the words blotted with drops of ink. He could not ask the secretaries or the typists, they did not come from his village, would not understand the scribe's handwriting, and spoke only English when they could. He followed the postman on his rounds of the college grounds, the principal's office, the various engineering departments, the mess halls, the hostels named for peaks in the Himalayas—Kanchenjunga, Everest, Godwin-Austen, Kailash—and the professors' houses on campus. Finally, in the evening, as the postcard crumpled and smeared with sweat, taking pity on Nathan's pleading look, the postman hammered out the edges and read the writing in the village scribe's unformed hand. *We have a girl child, my respected husband. Only another girl child, but she is beautiful. If I may, I would like to call her Parvati.*

Nathan stood there, crushed of feeling. For this he had lowered his dignity all day long? The postman bared his teeth with a smile, still holding the postcard. He knew Nathan's two older children were also daughters. So he smiled as if to say that if he had got his *baksheesh* at Diwali as was only right, the seed Nathan sowed within his wife would have grown into a boy child.

"Come and eat," a voice says. His wife stands close by his shoulder, close enough that the pleats of her sari stray by his skin. It is the way she touches him when they are in public. Not for them the blatant holding of hands, or mingling of fingers, or even, God forbid, the meeting of lips in full sight of everyone on the streets as Nathan has seen in two of the English films screened on campus in the open-air auditorium. He suddenly remembers the films and wonders if Parvati, sheltered and cloistered by him and his wife, had seen them. Was that why she had been . . . so . . . ?

His voice is harsh. "Has *she* eaten?"

"Of course not," his wife says softly. "You know she will not eat before you. But your grandchild is fed. His little tummy is full; he is on his way to sleep." She speaks in a low voice, so that, close as they are to Swamy and his wife, they will not hear this conversation.

"How are you?" Swamy's wife yells as they pass by her, deliberately overloud. Nathan's wife ignores her.

They sit as usual on the front verandah, where everyone else can see them. Nathan's wife has spread a knitted jute *pai* on the concrete floor, and set out just one stainless steel plate and a steel tumbler with boiled water. This is because Nathan will eat alone—the women of his family have never joined him in the meal; they are there to serve him and then to eat after he has had his fill. Until the child Krishna came into his quarters, no one has eaten before Nathan in the house. Nathan's wife first dots the outer rim of his plate with a jaggery *payasam*, so that he does not start his meal without a sweetened tongue. Then she heaps a mound of steaming rice in the center, ladles *rasam* over it, asks him how much of the potato curry he wants. She settles against the wall, watching him as he eats, anticipating second helpings of this, less of that.

Nathan eats like a king, for in his house, he is a king. Even if he is only a peon at work. Even he is the father of only daughters.

After Parvati there were no more children, and over the years Nathan grew accepting of the girls. They were a burden to be sure, all together, without the relief of a son. If Nathan had had a son, that son's earned dowry would pay for his daughters' given dowry. To earn this large dowry, the son would have to be educated somewhat, and have a good job, perhaps a peon at a large bank with air-conditioning, or personal peon to the managing director of some big company. For many years Nathan would conjure these ghost visions of the successful son he never had. Nathan would even painstakingly do some of the calculations or go to the department secretary to ask humbly for her to do the math. First, he would estimate education expenditures for the son, and add a little bribe for getting him a good job because that was necessary and a fact of life. Then he would add two dowries for his two older daughters (Parvati was supposed to be the son, so she was not counted in these grandiose schemes). The secretary would tell him what the total was and Nathan would add an extra ten percent to that amount for incidental expenses (one could never tell what Nathan might encounter as the children were growing up, the wretched girls might fall, or burn themselves in a kitchen fire, or some other demand would be made on his earnings).

The total was a very nice sum and eased Nathan's burdens for many hours.

When in these reveries, he forgot that Parvati was their third child; and after that Nathan's wife would not let him come near her without a condom, the chance of a son in their future be damned. He tried to reason with her, but *her* reasoning made more sense than his—she was tired of having children, saving for three dowries was enough, three was enough. Even the government said so. At this, Nathan stayed his arguments, for everywhere he went in the city, the government had family planning boardings picturing two adults and two children. "We are two, we have two." Nathan and his wife already had three. But three girls? Even the government would pity him. Surely. He was being made to pay for some sin he had committed in a previous life.

Nathan waits for the rice to cool on his plate, separating the grains so that the steam escapes from between them. He nods and his wife adds a dollop of curds on the rice, and another one, and yet another, until he holds his left hand flat across his plate, palm down, to say that it is enough. Nathan never speaks during his meals, and his wife does not expect him to. Instead she talks, feeding him little bits of gossip from the barracks, the happenings of their household, what the girls did, what they said.

In the last three years, she has suddenly become mute, for she is unable to talk of their grandchild to him. She knows

Nathan disapproves so greatly that she is afraid the food will curdle in his stomach if she mentions the child. But they live in two rooms, the child has been tottering around them, his little cries of joy and his tantrums fill the air—how does one ignore this? Pretend it does not exist? She sighs as she puts a piece of mango pickle next to the curds and rice. The mango piece falls from the spoon and small flecks of oil splatter on Nathan's rice. His hand stops on its way to his mouth but he does not look up at his wife. Even that small action is a reprimand in itself. She busies herself with asking if he wants more curds, more pickle, more of anything. He grunts and at that moment, his grandson wails in the room.

Nathan and his wife hear Parvati rise from her place in the other room and rush to her son. She croons to him. *"Jo, jo, raja."* Sleep, my king. When she says that word, *raja,* her voice cracks and falls into a silence, but they can still hear her pat the child back to sleep. Nathan eats steadily, wiping his plate clean, licking his fingers. His heart is laden with hurt at his daughter's slip of tongue in calling her son *raja.* For anyone else, this would be a common term of endearment, for her it is only shame. It is a pity, he thinks, that Parvati was not born a son—then none of this would be happening. Why, in the early years there had been nothing to indicate that such misfortune would befall them.

Even as his head filled with unfulfilled son dreams after Parvati's birth, Nathan worked very hard at his job at the

Department of Electrical Engineering, and was always respectful to the professors. Their wives hired him in the evenings and on weekends when there was a function or a festival in the house. On the bicycle that the college had given him, he rode to the vegetable *mandi* early every morning for one professor's wife who had fought with the grocer who wheeled his cart into the campus. Nathan took the bus to the train station to greet their relatives holding cardboard placards with names scribbled on them that he could not decipher. One professor did not send his children to the campus school, preferring a convent instead, so Nathan brought them back every afternoon by autorickshaw. Although he was long past his gardener status, he weeded gardens, mowed lawns, and with his meager carpentry skills even made tables and chairs on order. Nathan's wife worked as a maid, sweeping and mopping houses, cooking at times, washing clothes and vessels.

The three girls went to the campus school. By then, Nathan did most of his outside work for the wife of one professor in the department, Mrs. Rao. She told him that his daughters had to go to school, so he sent them, watching the money he had saved for their dowries dissipate into textbooks, pencils, school uniforms. What use was it to educate girls? He had himself never learned to read and write too much and yet he managed at his job well enough. All the girls were fit for was to cook and clean and bear children. His wife could teach them that.

So at first, Parvati's very presence was painful to Nathan,

thinking as he did of the son she should have been. Later, he began to see that what his wife had said in the postcard was true. Parvati was a beautiful child. Her two older sisters were regular hoydens in some senses, too attentive to themselves. They preened in front of the cracked mirror in the second room before school each day. Their uniforms needed to be starched and ironed. Their hair had to be well oiled, neatly plaited down their backs, one curl imprisoned and stuck to the sides of their cheeks. They painstakingly outlined their eyes with kohl. The *pottus* on the center of their foreheads were dabbed on with one finger dipped in glycerin, then with a dusting of red vermilion to form a perfect large circle. Jasmine flower garlands, measuring two elbow lengths, were pinned to the back of their heads. These two girls were so careful of their appearance that they would return home from school with their faces as though freshly done, not one hair awry, not one smudge on their skins, skirts still holding pleats as though they had not sat down during the day.

But Parvati was different from her sisters, and this Nathan saw when he allowed himself to take notice of her, and when his son fantasies seemed unlikely to come true. She did not have her sisters' obsessions with themselves. She would rise early in the morning too, but to sit on the verandah outside, to play with the pariah dog in the compound, to tease the squirrels and crows with nuts and tamarind fruit. Then five minutes before she had to go to school, with his wife yelling at her, Parvati would don her uniform, comb her long hair and plait it speedily, and run out of the house to catch up with her sisters. By the time she returned home the jasmine pinned to her plaits would be brown with age, her hair would be flying about her face, her shirt would be untucked from her skirt, and mud would ride up her shoes and socks, turning them a dull brown. She did not seem to care about this.

Over the years the girls grew up. They did not study beyond eighth standard; Nathan would not allow it, no matter what Mrs. Rao said. It was easy for her to say things like daughters should be educated and that she educated her one daughter. But Nathan saw that Mrs. Rao's son went to college on the campus, to get a degree in engineering; her daughter just did a BSc in some science subject in a Chennai college. And then she was married to a doctor in the city. In Mrs. Rao's world, her daughter had to have a college degree to be married. In Nathan's world, if his daughters were too learned, they would not find a husband. Eighth standard was enough, and they could even read and write and speak some English.

The two older girls were married to alliances that came from Nathan's home village. Good alliances, considering that he had only daughters, for even *that* fact was a strain on marriage negotiations. Prospective in-laws had hummed and muttered at his fate; asked if the other girls were married, if they had had their children already, all the while really asking *how much left over for this daughter, this girl you are offering us?* One boy was even a bank clerk. It was more than Nathan could have hoped for, and the dowry he paid for that daughter was twice the other's.

Then only Parvati was left at home with them. When she finished her schooling (at thirteen), Nathan put her to work at Mrs. Rao's house, the same work his wife did—cooking and cleaning and washing clothes and vessels. This Parvati did well, her hands fluid as she worked, a song lilting under her breath. She was a quiet child, did not speak much to her father or her mother, listened to them when they said something. She rose in the morning at six, went to work, came home to cook the lunch meal, and went back in the afternoon for two more hours of work. As she grew older, Nathan said she should come back to the barracks before the sun set, and obedient to his wishes, she did so.

Nathan washes up over the dirt around the verandah, leaning over the perimeter of concrete as his wife upends a brass *chombu* filled with water over his hands; eventually, she asks, "Enough?" in a sharp-edged tone. She has also heard the word *raja* from her daughter's mouth, and everything she forced herself to forget has returned.

A shouting rage rises within Nathan because she dares to take her dissatisfaction out on him. He struggles to retain the shreds of his shattered dignity. He has never had to raise his voice at his wife, beat his daughters, lower himself by making noise in front of the others in the barracks. Well, only once he had to, but that was an anger like none else—it had swept through his blood, set him on fire, nearly killed him.

He ignores his wife, ponderously silent as he pads down the verandah steps to the bottommost one, where he sits down. His wife brings him the *vetalaipaak,* and dutifully makes up a parcel of betel leaves and nuts. Nathan wedges the *vetalaipaak* between his back molars and his cheek and sucks the leafy juice into his throat. When the betel has softened and leaked out all of its redness, he will move it between his jaws, chew out the last of the juice, and then spit it out.

By now, almost everyone in the barracks is outside on the verandah, squatting over their own steps, separated from one another by a few yards at most, but they all look ahead into the darkness of the tamarind tree, and if they talk, it is with low nighttime voices, fatigued and musical.

Vikram, the sweeper in their barracks, had only one child, a boy named Raja, born a few months before Parvati. When Raja was born, Vikram went to the sweetshop outside the campus and bought *jangiris* for all of them. Eat, he had said, eat and make your mouths honeyed to fete the birth of my child. Nathan and his wife had obediently followed his instructions, and at the time, Nathan waited for his wife's round belly to give him a son. He had already decided what he would buy at the sweetshop—*gulab jamuns* bursting with sugar syrup, *aappams* that flaked and melted to the touch, and *palgova* so thick and creamy it could be fed with a finger. No mere *jangiris* for *his* son.

And this child Raja, called a king in the sweeper's quarters, became Parvati's favorite playmate. He had a mischievous face, thick swathes of hair that curled over his forehead, black eyes like an imp, a constant smile. When they were young, Parvati and Raja were inseparable, running to each other when they awoke, sitting together shoulder-by-shoulder, climbing the tamarind tree, fighting with the other children, defending only each other. Raja went to the campus school too, but all the way until twelfth standard.

In the beginning, Nathan did not like this friendship between Parvati and Raja, mostly because Vikram was a sweeper. His wife told him to let the children be, they were young, they knew little of these class distinctions. But even his wife did not like it much, Nathan knew, for she would keep Parvati indoors when their relatives from the village came to visit and only let her out when they had left, so they could not see who she associated with.

When Raja finished his school, the Department of Mechanical Engineering hired him as a peon. Just like that, no trials as sweeper or gardener or watchman—he went directly to peon, albeit a junior peon. It galled Nathan, but what could he do about it, other than watch Vikram gloat with pride at his son's position in life?

In these last years of Parvati's working and Raja's going to finish his schooling, a change had come over both of them. As was only right, Nathan decided. They were growing up, children no longer, and it would not have been correct for them to play together as they once had. Parvati was suddenly shy of Raja, and Nathan watched with foreboding as her eyes would glance to the left, toward Vikram's quarters, flushing when Raja came out whistling a film song. She had never learned to contain her emotions; in that she was still a child, presenting a naked face to the world, hiding nothing.

And then for the first time in almost all the years that they had been married, Nathan and his wife had a conversation. This was not just a command from Nathan to his wife, a comment from her to him—this was an exchanging of views. For in Nathan's world, the rules were so simple an idiot could understand them. Men and women married for convenience; if a child were ill, they talked about doctors or medicines; when a child was to be married, the man's opinion held sway on the rightness of alliances. And for his part, he never interfered in the cooking, although he had the authority to ask for specific dishes to be cooked, and to his liking. But now, with Parvati, Nathan was suddenly bereft, and wanted counsel even from his wife. Because there was no one else he could really turn to.

He and his wife talked at night, when they were sure Parvati was asleep. There could be no alliance between Parvati and Raja. It would simply not do. Not just for the class matter, but also they were of a different caste. For Nathan this was very important. It defined who he was, and stepping out of the caste was something only the rich and famous and indifferent did. Something Mrs. Rao would have blithely done—if such an opportunity for riches through marriage had presented itself to her for either her daughter or her son—and have passed it off as being modern and living with the times.

Parvati and Raja seemed to keep away from each other, as though knowing what their parents wanted. But Nathan's dislike of Raja grew to a loathing. He was an arrogant young man, and his mouth was constantly pursed in a whistle, until the sound frittered away Nathan's nerves. Raja's body was compact, his stomach flat with youth. His eyes were too hot, his childhood smile lingering in them when he looked at Parvati. And Nathan saw his daughter glance back, wistfully sometimes, when sweat drenched the back of Raja's khaki polyester uniform and defined muscles along his spine. For one year, they looked at each other. Just that.

"Appa." Parvati's voice is barely audible over the sound of the crickets chirping in the tamarind tree.

"What is it?" Nathan asks grimly.

"Amma forgot to give you some *payasam*. Here." She proffers a steel cup with the warm *payasam,* and then, when Nathan does not move, brings her arm around into his field of vision. That hand trembles suddenly, and the *payasam* slops around in its container. The glass bangles on her wrist meet in a tinkling sound.

In the beginning, Nathan would not even allow her to

call out to him with that word, Appa. Father. In the beginning, he would not talk with her, or acknowledge that she was there. He had held himself rigid with distaste when he heard her voice or saw her, frowned when she spoke, never met her gaze, never even looked at her. It was two years before Nathan could look upon his daughter Parvati again. And when he did, the roundness of her face surprised him. He had thought the immense tragedy that had befallen them, because of her, wretched girl, would have thinned her cheeks, laid hollows under her eyes, created the gauntness of guilt. But no, Parvati looked the same as she had, placid and content, the child Krishna in her lap, her smiles disappearing into her ears when she looked upon him.

There was something endearing about that smile to Nathan, much as he tried to argue himself out of it. And so little by little, he had begun to talk to her again. In commands mostly. Heat water for my bath. Or, Go call your mother. Or, Take that bawling child away. She blossomed under even so little an affection from him, and his heart filled to choking with grief again. Why, he had thought. Why.

"Appa." This time Parvati's voice is bold. "I heated the *payasam* again. Drink it soon, or it will cool and you will not like it."

Nathan eyes the cup, held in front of him with a hand that shakes no longer. The bangles are stilled of their clinking music, the forearm is steady, muscled. Parvati has thick hands and stubby fingers and a layer of grit decorates the edges of her short fingernails. She wears a cheap imitation gold ring on the little finger of her right hand. Nathan never bought her gold jewelry as he did for his other daughters when they got married; he never even gave her new clothes when Krishna was born.

He accepts the cup with a grunt and drinks the *payasam* through the left side of his mouth, away from the *vetalaipaak* stewing on the right side, tucked over his gums. The sweetness of jaggery, mashed *dal,* cardamom, and boiled milk soars over his tongue, and he thinks suddenly that the *payasam* has never tasted so good before.

"Where is he?" he asks, as he returns the cup to Parvati.

She takes a long time to answer, and what her expression is, Nathan cannot tell, for he still sits facing out into the yard, with his back to her. But it is the first time he has asked after the child; the very first time he has admitted to the boy's presence.

"Asleep," she says. "He has eaten well for his night's meal. Now he sleeps, my Krishna."

"Go," Nathan says, as an immense fatigue comes over him. He lights a *beedi* and smokes it in silence, waiting for Parvati to leave. She does walk away eventually, the long pleats of her sari whispering on the concrete floor. The sound scratches on Nathan's eardrums. She is too young, he thinks, to have graduated already to a sari, because of that child Krishna—because he made her a mother.

While it has been somewhat easy to ignore Parvati in the last two years, the child has infringed upon Nathan with his singing voice, his howls of imagined pain, his concentrated reciting of the nursery rhymes that Parvati has taught him. And then there were those unguarded moments when Nathan would feel a tiny hand tugging at the border of his *veshti,* or look up when the boy clasped his arms around Nathan's knees as he laboriously read the Tamil newspaper. Then all he could do was to shout for his wife, or more lately for Parvati, and say, "Remove him. Now."

When Parvati has gone back to the kitchen to wash and put away his *payasam* cup, Nathan begins to breathe again, until the ache blankets and smothers him. He rubs a hand over his chest, hoping to ease the pain. For three years this despair has persisted within him. When will it finally leave? When will he be free? Why had he not been more aware of what was happening with his daughter? But all Raja and Parvati had done was to glance at each other with an immense yearning.

Nathan went to speak with Vikram. This must not go on, he said of the atmosphere of longing. Vikram knew, and he knew that no marriage could come of this.

"But what to do, sir?" Vikram asked, his tone respectful, though laid under with a lightly mocking mirth. He did not have to worry too much, he had a son. A male child could do no wrong. If anyone had to be protected, it was Nathan's daughter, and that was not Vikram's problem. They smoked a *beedi* together, sitting outside the barracks on their haunches. This was the first and only time Nathan talked publicly with

Vikram. "Get your Parvati married, sir," Vikram said. Nathan nodded and went away, thinking about what the sweeper had said.

For the next few months, his wife and he cast around for alliances—from the village, from the neighboring barracks, and even from the Tamil newspaper's matrimonial advertisements section. But nothing came through, mostly because they did this desultorily, without too much enthusiasm. The reasons were myriad. Suddenly, they were both afraid of a house without a child, so used were they to having a third person around. And Parvati brought in some money from her maid's work. And the older daughters (and these were expected events) had children from their marriages. With each child, they came back to the barracks for their confinements and so there were hospital bills, doctor fees, new clothes for each birth, gold bangles for the babies, amulets of gold to be strung on black rope around the babies' waists to ward off the evil eye. It was, Nathan thought, an unending penance for having had daughters.

Then Raja got a new job—the job Nathan had coveted for his ghost son—as a peon for the managing director of a local foundry. He left the barracks and went to live in his own quarters in the city. A sudden space formed around them all and Nathan breathed more easily, did not dread returning home after a day's work, did not have to anticipate trouble. Parvati moped. Her eyes grew heavy with almost constant tears, and she took to refusing food, eating only sparingly, until she grew thin and wasted. Nathan's wife worried about her, retreating into an unnatural silence. But Nathan did not see the gloom over their quarters. He did not see, although he should have, that Parvati wore her thick-skirted *pavadai* higher and higher on her waist, covering something. Six months passed and one day, Nathan saw Parvati put a hand to her aching back as she squatted on the floor chopping up a cauliflower for curry. It was such a simple gesture, that massaging touch to the back, but one thronging with meaning.

His heart stopped and then flooded back into action. How? Where? When? Why did this have to happen to him? He ran to Parvati and grabbed a handful of her hair. Lifting her by her hair until the skin peeled away from her skull, he slapped her. Over and over again. Witch. Bitch. How could she? Nathan's wife came running out of the other room and shoved him against the wall. Please. Let her be. She did not know what she was doing. How could she have known?

He turned on her, enraged. She knew. She had known and not told him. He slapped his wife, knocked Parvati down, rained blows on her. Nathan's wife heaved herself up and covered her daughter. Don't, she yelled. You cannot hit her when she is in this condition. Think of the child. Think of her, think of *your* child.

"She is no longer my child." Nathan kicked at his daughter's legs, pulled his wife away, and dragged his daughter out to the verandah and to the gate near the tamarind tree. "Get out! I don't ever want to see you again. Get out and stay out."

By this time, the barracks were full of the others, leaning out of their windows, filling the verandah, watching goggle-eyed. Someone ran to Mrs. Rao, who left her dinner and came in a hurry. "Nathan, stop this!" she shouted.

Nathan was so saturated with rage that his limbs shook violently, and when he could not hit Parvati, he began to bang his fist into the bark of the tamarind tree's trunk until his fingers were bloody. And then, finally, his anger abated, his hands began to flare with pain, and the shivering stopped.

With one hand, Mrs. Rao waved the others back to their quarters and took a weeping Parvati indoors. The girl was bleeding from her head where her father had kicked her; Nathan's wife had a scraped elbow. Nathan sat outside, smoking *beedi* after *beedi* into the night, lifting a blood-caked hand to his mouth. Mrs. Rao came out and without a word went back to her house. She did not even look at him.

He sat there all night, weighted down by all that had happened, even his anger. He had never struck any of his children before. The lights stayed on in his quarters, and from time to time he saw his wife and Parvati look out of the window at him. As the sun glowed in the eastern sky, Nathan cried. At first he sobbed softly, tears running down his face, drenching the *beedi* end. Then out loud, hopelessness racking his body. Then he was enraged at Raja, at Vikram, a tough, surging anger that swamped through him. He rose and went to Vikram's door, demanded that Raja come from the city to marry his daughter. It was the right thing to do.

Suddenly, Vikram was no longer respectful. All night he had waited for this conversation, from the time he had watched Nathan beat Parvati. He said little, only this: "Is it really Raja's, Nathan? How do we know? How do we know anymore of anything? Is it really Raja's?"

After that day, Nathan grew densely quiet within himself. Mrs. Rao finally talked to him and told him he must look after Parvati. Somewhere within his heart, Nathan agreed with her. But how did she know how he felt, how could she even begin to see his pain? Of Raja, there was no news, no indication even that he had once lived in their barracks. He was gone, had disappeared into the city of ten million, not to be seen again. Nathan sent Parvati to the village to have the child. A few months after it was born, she came back to them. For there was nowhere else she could go, no one else whose name she bore, but Nathan's.

And slowly this child, this Krishna Shiva-Rama-Lakshman, pervades their lives. With his laughter; his shock of curly hair; his little, lithe body; his melodious voice. Parvati still works for Mrs. Rao, but takes the child with her and sits him down in the kitchen with a few spoons and a stainless steel tumbler for toys. She comes back home with him on her hip, a hibiscus bloom plucked from the Department's garden tucked behind his ear.

Behind him, Nathan strains to listen to the voices of his wife and his daughter. They have finished washing the vessels, now they wipe the plates, tumblers, and cups and stack them in the cupboards. What are they talking about? Where does Parvati find this vast courage? Why does nothing daunt her? She has returned from the village with an inner calmness as though she has done nothing to be ashamed of.

She does not look anymore toward the left, where Vikram lives. It is as though they do not exist, even though the child carries Raja's face. A year ago, Raja married some girl. The wedding was not here in the barracks. Nathan never sees Parvati pine for him.

She never seems to give a thought to herself either. This child she has borne, this Krishna she named after a god, has effectively banished all chance of a normal life for Parvati. There will be no marriage or future children for her—for who would marry a woman who has had a child out of wedlock, while her neck was still bare of the marriage *thali*? What will she do when Nathan and his wife are no longer alive, or too old to look after her? Nathan's head spins with these questions that have no agreeable answers, and now this is all he thinks about.

As he sits outside his barracks, still holding the *beedi,* he feels a touch, like a butterfly settling on his shoulder. It is Krishna, sleep heavy on his eyes, his hair tousled. He has crept out of his bed and walked to the verandah in search of his mother. He does not see her, but he sees his grandfather. He leans against Nathan's stiff back, and then moves around him to sit, puts his head in his lap. "Tha-tha," he says, haltingly. Grandfather. The first time he has used this word, although Nathan has heard Parvati teach him many times, pointing to Nathan's silent figure on the verandah steps.

For the first time, Nathan also sees Parvati's sweet face in the child. Her eyebrows, thick and meeting in the middle; her smile, her lips, not Raja's. Nathan throws away the *beedi;* his hands hang by his side. He does not know what to do with them. Krishna looks up at him. Slowly, Nathan smoothes the hair from his forehead and pats him on the chest as he has seen Parvati do. *"Jo-jo,"* he rasps, his voice unused to these words of petting. *"Jo-jo, kanna."* Sleep, my love. Krishna closes his eyes.

A few minutes later, Parvati comes rushing out of the quarters, trembling with worry. She stops when she sees them, her child with his head in her father's lap. The tears on her father's face, his hand caressing Krishna's hair.

The Key Club

*O*n this night, once every four months, they change their names to Ram and Sita. They begin to think of themselves by these names from the moment the servant maid knocks on their bedroom door at ten A.M. and says, *"Kapi thayaar."* Coffee is ready. The club always meets on a Saturday night, and on Sunday, Ram and Sita each go to their yoga class, their meditation class, the five-star gym at the Temple Palace Hotel with its shimmering Olympic-sized swimming pool, and end the day with a Laugh Class in Clyde Park where they learn to laugh from the bottom of their bellies until their eyes tear up.

The membership into the Key Club was Ram's idea; Sunday's schedule is Sita's. "It centers us," she had said. Ram has always been "centered," well, around himself anyway, so the classes are unnecessary for him. He could say, Come on, Sita, we're Indian, no necessity to indulge in New Age stuff to make us feel . . . more oriental. He gives in, however, graciously; Sita obviously needs the centering more than he does. On Monday, and every day after, until the next club meeting, their lives follow an unaltered routine.

The children have long been awake when the maid scrapes at the door to their bedroom. Ram woke first at eight o'clock and heard his son shout for his milk. The maid's voice answered, and then he heard a cooing as his son drank, singing behind the sips of milk.

"What will you do until the evening?" Ram asks, lifting his head from his pillow to look at his wife.

"Get ready," she says.

"You are beautiful today," he says. And he means it. He and his wife keep different hours. He comes home late from work, sometimes at ten o'clock in the evening, sometimes later, and the children are usually in bed by then. Sita will be watching a television show or reading a book; she has already eaten her dinner.

There is little that passes for conversation between them, because they have very dissimilar interests. The television does not interest Ram, neither do movies; he lives so much in himself, in the present, that he cannot manage even the smidgen of credulity it requires to watch other people's (fictionalized) lives and perhaps project their cares and worries onto his own. He has never read a book in his life. This is not an entirely true statement, of course—Ram has a master's degree in mechanical engineering from the United

States; a bachelor's degree in engineering from a local Chennai college; a school passing certificate from Bledsoe Academy ("Only the best go to Bledsoe")—somewhere in all that schooling Ram has read a book, a textbook only, perhaps, but a book. Until a few years ago, Ram would proclaim with some pride, "I have never read a book in my life. And I don't intend to spoil my streak."

The statement, delivered as it was, among his friends, or acquaintances who had similar interests (or were in the mood to be adoring of Ram), was met, as it was expected by him to be met, with laughter and a crack about "How funny, *yaar*—what a riot you are. What about an instruction manual?"

"Why?" Ram would say lazily. "I have enough people to set up anything I want set up, operate it, and fix it when it's broken." This would be followed by a silent and long sigh, sometimes filled with envy. And then Ram said this at a dinner that his parents were hosting at the Gymkhana Club a few years ago.

They were twelve at the table, the dinner had been cleared away, Sita was delicately scraping the last of the mango ice cream from the white bowl in front of her, a few of the men and some of the women had leaned back in their chairs to light cigarettes. The usual laughter followed, somewhat muted and not as idolizing (these were his parents' friends—they didn't feel compelled to applaud his efforts), but from the person Ram had most hoped to impress, there was a raised eyebrow and a look of such incredulity that he felt himself flush. Seated across from him was the guest of honor of the evening, a woman who wrote novels about something, he couldn't remember what. He had asked, and he remembered that she had answered him, her voice falling into silence when she realized that he wasn't paying attention to her, only to the curve of her neck. She hadn't even looked at him since. And people didn't normally ignore Ram, not for long, anyhow. He was a handsome man. His hair crowned his head in thick and loose curls, his smile captured everyone, his body was slender and long and he towered over crowds. Women liked him. They liked his height, they liked his broad hands, and they liked his sense of humor. If his sheer beauty and appeal could be ignored, very few could pass by his lineage.

Ram's great-grandfather had begun a small automotive company in the early 1900s with his fishing profits. To begin with, it was little more than a garage with one mechanic who knew how cars worked. Most of the business came from bicycle repairs. Today, Shiva Motors sold tires; rebuilt engines; manufactured scooters, bicycles, and mopeds; and dealt in car sales. Ram's mother was the fourth daughter of the current ruling house and had a tenth of a share in the company. They owned three houses in the city and one in the hill station of Ooty. Ram had traveled around the world twice already—once when he was ten years old as a birthday present from his parents, and once when Sita and he went on their honeymoon, another gift from his parents. Ram worked in the company as one of the directors. No one could easily disregard the weight of all this favor visited upon Ram. But the novelist had.

Sita had laughed, Ram remembered, at the novelist's reaction to Ram's statement that he had never read a book. It wasn't anything overt, nothing anyone else had picked up on at the table, but Ram knew Sita had laughed, when she held the last of her mango ice cream on a spoon at the very tip of her luscious tongue and deliberately closed her mouth around it. Ram never repeated this statement again in public. In time, he forgot that he used to say it. It began not to matter anymore.

The children come in for their morning playtime. They jump on the bed between Ram and Sita, they squeal for a while; the maid watches them anxiously from the door to the bedroom awaiting a signal from either of them to take the children away.

For a week before the club meeting, Sita keeps away from Ram, and he lets her be. The asceticism suits him also. He revels in the constant longing, waking nights to her beside him, once even touching her hip under the covers only to have her breathing tense. She makes no mention of that touch in the morning. So by the day of the club meeting, Ram's senses are wild and on edge; to keep them thus, he eats very little all through the day. A boiled egg and half a slice of toast for breakfast. A cup of *dal* and a salad for lunch. He picks at his dinner. By nighttime, after two perfectly mixed gin and tonics, his body hums with anticipation. His mind is sharp and with his thoughts he reaches out where he wants, makes and wills things to go his way. They always have. On the club evenings, Ram has always acquired what he wanted.

The club was . . . someone's idea; Ram can no longer remember whose. There are eight of them in the club. They don't count their wives as members; their wives are guests. There is always the possibility that one of their marriages will not work out. Although that is much less of a probability than a possibility—they are all, in that sense, old-fashioned enough to think that they will remain married to these women until they die. Still, when they formed the club, they vested themselves only as the primary and sole members. Most of them are in their early thirties now—Vish is thirty-five, and he is the oldest member of the club. Ram, Jay, Dharma, and Sat are thirty-two. Vy, Alistair, and Arth are thirty-three.

None of the names are real, even as Ram is not his real name. But now he only thinks of them as such, by these names, because they no longer see one another in social gatherings, or invite one another home for dinners or go out for movies. All these casual engagements among the eight of them and their wives stopped a few months after they formed the club. Among the eight of them—well, among them and all of their parents—they own seventy-five percent of the city's wealth.

Ram has known Jay and Vish all of his life. He grew up on the street that led to the city's Boat Club, known eventually as Boat Club Road. Ancient rain trees cant over the tar road, creating a semipermanent and cool shade from the summer's heat. The houses lie behind whitewashed concrete walls; graffiti never mars their pristine fronts, since they all have a watchman at their iron gates. The driveways curve to the front of the houses. The verandahs have long and smooth white pillars. The windows have no metal grills, just plain and shiny glass hand-polished into a gleam by the maids every day. Inside, the mosaic floors shine, Persian rugs adorn hallways and drawing rooms, and when Ram was in high school, the top floor of his house echoed with the music of Pink Floyd from his Bang & Olufsen system. There was a brief Jethro Tull period in Ram's life, and another foray into hard rock with Deep Purple, but it is Pink Floyd Ram carries with him into his adulthood.

A car took his father to work. Three cars stood in the driveway with three drivers who waited until Ram, his mother, or his sister decided to go somewhere during the day. The drivers came to the house at five A.M. and left at ten P.M. each night, unless Ram chose to go to a party at Vish's or Jay's homes. Jay lived two houses down the street, toward the Boat Club; Vish lived three houses up the street. The car still took Ram to their houses and brought him back when he wished to come back. The next morning, the driver would be at the house again at five A.M.

He thought little about this lifestyle. He thinks little about this even now. After he leaves for work every morning, a car and a driver wait for Sita in their driveway; another car and driver take the children to school and come back home until it is time for them to return from school. There is nothing in life that Ram has wanted. Nothing he has not acquired when he has wanted it. It has been the same for Vish and Jay—these two whom Ram has known all of his life, with whom he has climbed the rain trees on the road, whose European travel stories so perfectly match his, who went to Bledsoe Academy with him and then to the engineering college in the city where they met the other five members of their club.

The one thing they all have in common is wealth. Of course. And it was easy enough, even in college during their undergraduate years, to see who had money and who didn't. The cars that brought them to their classes each morning were Mercedes-Benzes or Volvos. Sat's father owned a Maserati and only allowed him once, in the four years they spent at college, to drive it into the campus. All other times, he had to make do with a BMW. The poor chap. Ram thought that his father was an unfair man.

So their combined wealth, flaunted or not, brought the eight of them together. Vish lit the first joint that Ram smoked, late one night when they drove out to the campus and climbed the concrete bleachers in the stadium to huddle together at the top right corner. From here, they could see and not be seen. The grounds below were swathed in darkness, but as they became progressively and gently stoned, they saw a white dog cross the field, and the college phantom, a man with a limp and a scythe held on his shoulder, its curved edge around his neck. They both saw the man and watched him scuttle across the beaten mud *maidan* with its faint white running track lines painted in an oval.

Ram drove home that night in a daze. He thought he remembered being stopped by a policeman on Boat Club Road; the next morning, a policeman knocked at their gate, and his mother sent a maidservant out with five hundred rupees in a brown envelope. Ram never recalled what he hit on the road on his way back home. A dog? A cat? A . . . ? But he also never smoked a joint again.

He never smoked cigarettes (none of the eight members of the club smoked), he never drank in excess (even when he was in college), he never overate and became fat, and he never tried marijuana or any other drug again. He had the money; it was easily accessible. And that was the reason why Ram kept some virtues—there was never a curiosity in him for things that his money could buy. He suspected that it was much the same for the other members of his club. Wealth, power, position, prestige, privilege—they had it all, and they had all. Except . . . and so, they started the Key Club.

Ram spent two years in the United States acquiring an MS in mechanical engineering. His grades in college had been good; his GRE scores were actually almost perfect. He sat for the Advanced GREs in Mathematics and Physics and aced them both. For a lark, because he had little else to do the summer before he went to America, Ram took an AGRE in biochemistry, cell and molecular biology also, and scored spectacularly in it. He had wanted to be a doctor at one point, in tenth standard, and then gave up the wish to do so because it would involve far too much work. Sita found his biochemistry AGRE score sheet one day in his study and asked him, a look of puzzlement on her face, "Why?"

"I don't know why," Ram had replied. "Just because. I wanted to. I did well, you know."

She held the paper in front of him. "Obviously."

Ram was awarded a teaching assistantship at the U.S. university, which he refused. His parents paid for his MS degree. They also paid for his apartment, the furniture in the apartment, and the 1967 Chevy Camaro with a V-8 engine that Ram had painted indigo blue with thin pink stripes along the sides in a body shop. Ram opted for the university he went to because both Sat and Vish were there also. Summers, they dumped duffel bags with their clothes into the Chevy's boot and drove across the country, the windows rolled down, Pink Floyd on the music system, picking up girls where they stopped for the night. They came back to India with photos from Yellowstone, Mount Rushmore, and Yosemite. Ram also returned with a perfect 4.0 GPA for his graduate degree—Sat and Vish didn't do quite as well, but neither of them had gone to America to study. They had jobs waiting for them at home, regardless of how they spent their postgraduate years.

In college in the city, whether it was because of the Maserati or not, Sat was Ram's closest friend. They were both in mechanical engineering, both in the same year; both also looked alike with the same hand-on-hip stance when they were quizzical, a similar smile when they saw a girl they liked. And there was a girl they both liked very much in college. Her name was . . . well, her actual name doesn't matter, they call her Sara now.

Ram saw Sara first. She was a year older than them, also in mechanical engineering, and different from the girls they had known and dated before. Sara's parents did not have money, and that summed up the difference more accurately than anything else could. Sara was a serious, studious girl. She had long hair that she plaited down her back and thick eyeglasses that gave her a mild squint. She wore only *salwar-kameez* sets, rarely pants or skirts, and she took the city bus to college. She had a lovely, sweet voice, and this Ram and Sat heard for the first time when the principal of the college called Sara up onstage at the morning assembly to sing the national anthem when the regular singer was absent. They took notice then, glancing at each other during the anthem.

That afternoon, Ram passed Sara and a group of girls under the shade of a tree on campus and stayed there below the outermost fringe of the tree's leaves watching as a breeze brushed over her clothes, molding the thin cotton cloth to her breasts and her hips. She laughed and took off her glasses to wipe the laughter from her eyes. The wind swept gently over her hair. And Ram, who had never been denied anything in his life, went up to her, among her friends, and said, "Would you like to get a cup of coffee at the canteen with me?"

She said yes. Of course. But not before she had put her glasses back on and bowed her head in shyness. Ram was enchanted.

The next day, Sat said, "You took her first, you bastard." And that was all he said. Ram and Sara dated all through college, for the next three years.

The children leave the room and Sita rises from the bed to go to the bathroom. When they were first married, it was her walk that most irritated Ram, a sort of jerk and go, jerk and stop. Sita used to flail on high heels, pleading that she had never worn them before. Ram taught her how to walk, not just walk toward him, but walk away from him so that she captured his gaze and kept it. She uses it now, unconsciously graceful, loose-limbed from sleep, her hair cascading down her back. He likes watching his wife walk. Even at the club meeting, as she approaches the glass bowl with the keys, she walks so that no one can look away. Not just because of what she is about to do, but because they all either want her or want to be like her. And Ram has taught her this.

She is silent as she shuts the bathroom door. He will not hear her speak again today, and her first words to him will be tomorrow evening when he holds out his hand for her after the Laugh Class. He will say, "Coming home?"

And she will say, as she always says, "Sure."

Ram goes out of the bedroom to the guest bathroom for his shower and his shave. After breakfast, he calls the hotel to confirm the reservations. In the afternoon, he sleeps for an hour and plays solitaire for two.

When Ram left for his graduate degree in the United States, he also left Sara behind in India. Her parents couldn't afford the plane ticket and so she couldn't go to America even though she had a fellowship for a master's degree for a full two years. She found a job instead at a local company. When they broke up, it was almost as if she had expected it.

"You're going, aren't you?" she had said.

"And when I come back . . ." Ram shrugged. "Sorry."

"You aren't really coming back," she said. "I'm sorry too. I thought I knew you, Ram. But I think I know you only too well." And then she said, most astonishingly to him, "Good luck. With everything."

He had been almost shocked by those words. He had never needed luck in his life. He had money. He could not marry her because he would marry money. Dating in college was fine, but marriage . . . it was a practical institution. His mother had married his father for a reason, well, several, of which could be counted money, power, family name, and some itinerant dabbling in local politics that also translated into money, power, and family name. His uncles and aunts had done the same. His sister was already married to a shifty-eyed man who could not keep his pants zipped. But he had money . . . and the rest of it.

When Ram, Sat, and Vish returned to India, they started to work in their parents' companies. Ram's mother had told him that he must work for at least a year before he could get married, and he agreed. It was his time for freedom. When the year passed, his mother brought Sita to the house one evening with her parents. They were of old money. And their wealth came from property—a hundred thousand acres of prime, arable land in the delta of the state's biggest river; irrigation was never a problem, there was plenty of water, and there were no fickle monsoons to rely upon. They had a sprawling house at one edge of the property, with brilliant green lawns, lush palm trees, peacocks in the gardens. They had three hundred in-house servants.

But for that walk, that stumbling, childlike walk, Sita was beautiful. She was fair, she had huge eyes, she had dimpled elbows with smooth, smooth skin. She had three sisters, all younger than her, and the moment Ram and Sita married, two more were married off to equally prosperous sons-in-law.

Ram and Sita had their first child twelve months after the wedding, the second came along three years later. Both were boys. By the fifth year of their marriage, Sita had lost ten kilos, played tennis with the marker at the Gymkhana Club, spoke English fluently (more fluently than she had before in her country and village upbringing), and learned to walk toward and away from the members of the Key Club without tripping once in three-inch-heels from Italy.

That was a few years before the Key Club was formed.

The only time Ram ever felt a want, or perhaps a betrayal, was the year that he had returned home to India to work at his mother's company as a (beginning) Managing Director. The year he was to wait until his mother found him Sita. He had thought about Sara a lot in the first few months, wondered where she was, if she was married, to whom, what she looked like now . . . if her singing voice sounded the same. And then, a few months later, he had come upon her in a restaurant, clad in a lavish silk sari, a necklace of diamonds around her neck, diamonds in her ears, gold bangles tumbling down her slender arm. Her eyebrows were cleanly arched above eyes that sparkled—contact lenses, Ram thought, why had she not worn them in college?

He rose from his table and went to greet her, and felt a sense of shock as the man seated next to her turned and showed him a laughing profile as he touched Sara upon the shoulder with a settled hand. It was too intimate a gesture in public for it to mean anything other than what it was. That man was her husband. And that man was Sat.

"Dude!" Sat said, turning to him. "I married her, you see? You left her, I married her."

And he had always wanted her, Ram thought. Even when Ram and Sara had been dating. Though not once, and he cast his mind back deliberately to ponder on this, not once had there been even an ounce of impropriety in Sat's behavior toward Sara when they were in college. But since, yes, since there had been.

They told him of their two-year correspondence through letters, emails, and phone calls when Ram, Sat, and Vish had been in the United States. Sara mentioned the trip to Yellowstone, the photos of them in front of enormous brown bison, their backs to the animals as they posed with fingers splayed in a V for victory sign. "How silly of you," she said. "You might have been gored if the bison had so chosen."

Silly, Ram thought. He had been silly. He wondered then if she had felt a pang of longing when she saw him in the photos, or if he had been let go as easily as . . . he had let go of her. But standing there, looking down upon the two of them, married a mere six months, Ram knew that he had been not just silly, but outrageously stupid. He was in love with Sara. But still, the Key Club, when it came into being, was not Ram's idea, but Sat's.

Ram and Sita drive to the hotel in silence. They leave the children in the middle of a fight—between the two of them, that is—and leave the maid to sort it out, to hush their tears, to feed them their dinner and put them to bed. As it is almost every evening whether they are at home or not. As it was, Ram thinks as they wait for a light to turn green, when he was growing up. His mother always wore her hair short, a boy-cut they called it then, and now. Clipped around her ears, a razor edge at the back, a slop of hair over her forehead. One of the things he had been grateful for in both Sara and Sita was that they had long, old-fashioned hair, in Sara's case, hitting the back of her knees. Sita has long since cut her hair to fall just below her shoulders, layered and styled into loose waves. Tonight, she wears a simple pink chiffon sari, a wisp of a blouse with two strings across the back, silver high heels, and a pair of silver hoops in her ears.

Pink Floyd's "Money" booms softly on the car's CD player. Ram feels like singing along, but he is quiet. And then Sita says, "Why did you ever form this damned club?"

He brakes suddenly and horns blast out at him. The windows are rolled up against the summer night, but he can still hear an autorickshaw driver as he leans out from under the canvas awning of his vehicle and shouts, "Yo, did ya warn them at home before you left, stupid?"

A common slang-curse—did you tell your dear ones before you left home that you were planning on dying today? Stupid.

"A damned club?" he says. "You seem to like it well enough."

"And so do you."

Yes, he thinks. "Who will you . . ." He stops, unable to ask anything further, and sees a little smile lift the edges of her mouth. It is that smile, that non-smile, that knowing light in her eyes when she does this that made Sat want to form the club.

A couple of years ago, the eight of them had gone out for dinner at a gentlemen's lounge. They had watched as the slender, black-clad waitresses had leaned over their shoulders to place plates in front of them, cleared the food away, brought them more drinks, asked if they wanted *anything* else. As the evening progressed the women seemed to touch them more often, a sliding rub on the shoulder, a bump from a toned hip, a flip of long, straight hair.

Sat had said, a bemused look on his face, "There's no one quite like your wife though, Ram. You're a lucky bastard."

The others, Vish especially, had agreed, raising their glasses in a silent toast.

"So are you," Ram had said. "You married the girl I love."

In the present tense, and he thought they all realized it, but no one said anything.

And then Sat began a story about some friends of his in Mumbai who had formed something called a Key Club. The waitresses disappeared, the room grew quiet.

"What is the one thing we do not have?" Sat said. "The one thing money cannot buy for us? Something to think about, isn't it?"

They did. They thought about it that night when they returned home to their sleeping wives and children, to hushed houses, to clocks that chimed the hour. Ram called Sat the next morning and said that he was in. Over the next few days they all called Sat. Although they were to be the members of the club, it could not exist without their wives' consent. It took a year for all of the wives to agree. Sita was the last to submit. The club had met three times so far. Tonight is the fourth meeting.

There was one rule that had to be followed with diligence. The wives must not be influenced in their decisions; they must make their own picks, and they must be the ones to choose. Unsaid, and critical to the longevity of the club, was that the members of the club must accept whatever happened at the club meeting, and never talk about it.

"Why, Ram?" Sita asks again in the car as they approach the hotel.

So he tells her. And then, "Why ask now, Sita? You've been happy enough the last three times."

He lets that slip without meaning to, and remembers now that Sita had glowed on every post–Key Club meeting Sunday. Oddly, to Ram, because he would never have thought that Vish . . . if anything, it was Sat he was afraid of. Sat who had first said that Sita was lovely, Sat who had come up with the idea of the club, who hoped each time that he would be picked. Sat who had married the woman Ram is in love with. And on each occasion as the time for the picking came, there were two thoughts that warred constantly in Ram. Who would choose him, and who Sita would choose. Not Sat, he thought each time, not Sat.

"Ram and Sita," Sat says as they enter the private dinner lounge at the hotel. "You are late."

They are all there. All sixteen of them with their made-up names—so that they can be tonight what they aren't in their real lives. Ram chose their names for the Key Club after Ram and Sita from the *Ramayana*. A funny choice, Sita had said once, didn't Ram exile his wife to the jungle when she was pregnant with twins for the mere suspicion that she might have been unfaithful to him? And she had gone through an *Agni-Pariksha,* a literal trial by fire, walked through fire and come out unscathed to prove to him that she was still pure, still untouched by Ravana. What a fickle man he was, Sita had said. Funny you would choose his name for yours.

Ram hadn't thought that far into the story, of course. In his mind was a brief memory from when he was ten years old, peering around the door of the drawing room late one night during a party his parents had hosted, and Vish's father had passed behind his mother's chair and stroked her back with his gin and tonic glass. Ram's mother had shivered and bowed her head. Ram knew, and knew this with certainty only many years later, that Vish's father and his mother had been having an affair. What his father thought of this, or if he even knew or cared, Ram did not know. So when the club was formed, he changed their names to Ram and Sita—Ram who had fought the demon king Ravana who had captured his wife, rescued her, and brought her home with him safely. A few years later the god Ram had let his wife go, but Ram *really* hadn't thought that far into the story.

They are subdued tonight, the laughter is almost nonexistent, and they eat in silence, forks clinking on china plates. The lights dim when they finish eating. All the men reach into their pockets and bring out their car keys. Sometime, earlier in the evening, a waiter set a clear, cut-glass bowl in the center of the table, and all through dinner it sits sparkling in the muted light.

There are eight rooms booked upstairs in the hotel—each identical, dark teak furniture, creamy white bedspreads, a view to the blue-green swimming pool and the lawns. Eight rooms, and there are eight card keys on the table now, which Vish removed from an envelope and fanned out over the table. He then deposits his car keys into the bowl. Ram does the same, and watches as Sat puts his keys in also. Sat glances at Sita, but she is looking at the mirrored surface of the table and not at him.

The women draw lots from another envelope. Sita's number is seven. By the time her turn comes, Sara has already picked up Vy's car keys from the cut-glass bowl, and the only two women remaining are Sita and Alistair's wife. Sat and Vish are still unclaimed.

Ram's head throbs. Not Sat, he thinks. Don't pick Sat. The last three times, Sita chose Vish's keys—chose to go with him and the card key to a room upstairs, chose to spend all of that Saturday night with him. She came back home the next day lit from within with an inner fire of satisfaction. But it is Sat who wants Sita, who is so desperate to sleep with Ram's wife that he forms the club just for this chance that she might choose him also. Sat who stole Sara from Ram, and married her instead. Not Sat, please.

Sita reaches into the bowl, and her fingertips glow pink through the glass. When her hand comes out, she holds Vish's keys.

Bedside Dreams

I watch as Parvati bends over Kamal, lifting his arm to tuck the sheet around his body. Her movements are gentle, as though she takes care of a child. She smoothes the fabric over him, then reaches out to even the hair on his forehead. Her fingers linger on the side of his still face, as if to absorb his warmth. She does this for me, I know, for then she looks up and winks. I smile slowly as she leaves the room. My gaze comes back to Kamal and pain scuttles inside me. This once-vibrant man is an empty shape lying on pale sheets that overpower his skin. Veins stand out on the fragile face I once covered with kisses. Somewhere in the chest a tentative breath catches his lungs, fills them briefly, and then flees.

I remember leaning over my first daughter a few days after her birth to check if she was breathing. My fingers would meet the little throb on the side of her head, or I would hold my hand in front of her nose as her little breath condensed on my palm. This I did every night, many many times, waking from a deep sleep, feeling I must go to her. For Kamal, the man who gave me that daughter, I cannot do this. I can only watch over him. I can only guard him, knowing that inevitably one day even that shallow rise and fall of his ribs will stop.

This will last for a long time, they say. Why wait like this? Why stand vigil over an already empty bed? Do you notice, as you go through life, how many people think they have a say in it? How many people give you advice for various useless reasons? They've lived longer; they know better; they are just smarter. I, who have known this man more precisely than anyone else, can tell he will not last long. Until then, I will be here, by his side. And then he will be gone, his life extinguished after eighty-three years, sixty-seven of which we spent together, never apart for more than three days at a stretch.

I cannot talk to Kamal and I know he cannot hear me. In any case, we don't need words anymore. A glance, a raised eyebrow, a smile, these are enough for us to communicate with after so many years of marriage; and in the early, turbulent years, we rarely had the time for talk anyway. When I was pregnant with our first daughter, I spent one night in jail for demonstrating on the streets the night the Indian Congress passed the Quit India resolution. 1942. I was sixteen years old. As we demanded the British leave India, they swept us haphazardly into overfull prisons. By the next morning, they had started culling us out. I was let go first, my stomach round with the child, my face blanched from a sleepless night. Kamal, president of the local chapter of the Congress, had to stay in jail. Freed, he would create problems, for outside our little realm, beyond our burning purpose, the whole world raged in war.

I visited Kamal every day. We would sit on the floor at one end of the cell, leaning against the wall, iron bars separating us. But our shoulders touched, and if I leaned hard enough, I could put my head to his. For the next three years, Kamal made brief appearances at home, only to be yanked back to jail at the smallest pretext, sometimes leaving his dinner to cool as he left.

So when that child, our first daughter, was born in 1942, Kamal was still in jail. And when she died a month after her birth, Kamal still hadn't seen her, hadn't touched her. We have twelve other children. Now when all I do is wait, I wonder about the daughter who died, who we never named because I was waiting for Kamal to do so. I wonder if she would have been different.

My eyes cast over the chalky whitewashed walls within my range of vision and then to the beds lined in a military row along the sides of the room. Twelve to each side. This has been our home for the last twenty-three years, from the day Kamal retired from the Indian Railways as chief engineer.

I remember the day he was promoted from foreman to engine driver. He had come home, his face flushed and handsome, tripped over three of the children, patted them absently, and then hugged me and my growing belly in his warm arms. As the children watched round-eyed, we danced around the room, the one room we could afford to rent then, where we ate, and slept, and made love. But all that changed that day. We rented another room.

Kamal's job took him away from me more often now than before, but never for more than three days. Each time he left, I touched his face with cold lips and would not stop trembling until he returned. Such an attitude toward a husband was not healthy, they said, distance made a marriage work. *Love* was not a word to be used in public, rather to be implied—if I was asked whether I loved my husband, I must nod, or bow my head in agreement. But I must never love him too much—not enough to allow my whole self to be overcome by him. Before we were married, they came to me with advice. Listen to your husband, or pretend to do so, at least at first. He will do strange things to you under cover of darkness, but that is a woman's lot in life. And make sure you provide him with many sons, they said, daughters are a burden. The dowries, the uncontrollable and demanding in-laws, the constant fear of one of them being spoiled (through her effort or not)—daughters, they said, were like milk left out on the kitchen countertop overnight.

I had met Kamal only once before we were married—as was the custom—when he came to see me with his parents and the marriage broker. I was sixteen; it seems young these days when girls do not marry until they are finished with their college at least. But then, I was considered the right age for marriage—college was not possible (I had not even completed my schooling)—I was four years beyond puberty. Left alone too long without the tether of marriage, like the milk, I too might spoil. My mother made me dress up in a purple-and-gold silk sari she had kept for the occasion. I wore that sari three times, twice before Kamal came visiting. The other two times one prospective groom said I was too dark, the other thought me too tall. Kamal, no indecisive Goldilocks, found me just right. He later told me I glowed like a butterfly. I showed off my meager skills, twanging the *veena* strings until even my mother flinched, singing classical songs with a hoarse defiance until Kamal put a hand up to his mouth to hide a smile. My mother served them gold-tinted, saffron-scented *halwa* and lied as usual when she said I had made it. Kamal taught me to cook when we were married. But long before that, after he had said yes to me, there were tales of how I should be not just a good wife, but, eventually, a powerful one.

From our first time together I knew the advice to be useless. The hot, still nights under the clanking ceiling fan were welcomed, and during the days we would look at each other with a secret, precious laughter. It was as though I had lived my life in a vacuum for sixteen years—and then there was Kamal. Everything—every breath, every thought, every deed, every feeling—centered around him. The sons came, the daughters came, but my connection with Kamal flourished stronger every day. The children grew sturdy and strong and brilliant. I think we taught them to laugh, but they don't do so very often anymore. They say life was easier in our time. I wonder. I *know* we taught them to laugh, for we never stopped as time went by. Kamal's promotions came with an increasing regularity. The rooms of our houses grew. And all the boys eventually went to engineering college, except one who is a doctor. And the girls all married well. We have a lot of grand-children, how many, I could not say at this moment because we have not seen them in almost ten years.

The day after Kamal retired, we had to move out of our palatial white-pillared mansion courtesy of the Indian Railways. For months we had waited to hear from our sons, expecting each of them to insist that we stay with them. For months there was silence and I saw Kamal droop visibly. His hair suddenly became white, the lines on his face grew more pronounced, and his shoulders stooped as though he were carrying a large burden.

They say women are stronger than men. But each time I looked at Kamal, my heart broke. I kept my tears inside with a fierce pride. When neighbors, well-meaning or not, came to ask of our future, I laughed and made a joke about not being an encumbrance on our children, and they left, some with sympathy written over their faces, some with barely veiled contempt. I could almost hear them think. *Twelve children, so many sons, and nowhere to go? What a pity.* Finally, I searched for the courage to call my oldest son home one evening when Kamal was out, and asked him where we were going to live.

My heart burns even today when I think of that meeting. This boy I had cherished. He had come to us in 1947, the year India became independent. I know that after so much time few people remember those days of danger and heady joy. When freedom comes too easily it is not valued, but for us that year was important, because we were a free people, and because this son lived, whereas *she* had not.

Now our son sat in front of me, hemming and hawing about the inconvenience of having his parents stay with him. No place, he said at first, and they live in a six-bedroom house with quarters for a maid and a gardener. Too expensive, said our General Manager son, when Kamal would receive a large pension from the Railways for all his years of service. We were too liberal, said our son who beat his eighteen-year-old daughter with a broom for bringing her male classmate home for tea and biscuits. *Tea and biscuits.* This I still do not understand. Many years before this son was born, I stood by fiery youths and listened to Congress propaganda. I marched with them; I spent a night in jail with them. My reputation stayed intact. But in today's world, if I am to believe my son, no decent man will marry his daughter if she as much as spoke to a person of the male sex. And so he went on and on, one justification after another, while I listened in dulled silence.

His mouth moved in meaningless garble, and my mind floated back many years to when he was newly come to us. It had been five years since *her* death, that ink-haired child I had sung to sleep every night. Kamal had not let me bring her to see him. Not like this, he had said, not in jail. Let her see her father as she ought to, a free man, a victorious man. She never saw her father after all, only heard of him from me, in songs, in my prayers, in my voice. So when this boy was born, I reached trembling, yearning hands for him, thinking, let him live. They put him on my chest and I saw the tiny mouth move in protest, eyes shut against a new world, hands clutching at my skin for protection. I hugged him, wanting to guard him all my life.

But he was no longer that child. He sat in front of me, his stomach hanging over his too-tight belt, his face more wrinkled than mine, and I thought I did not know this stranger I turned to for help.

Then, for the first time, I wondered if Kamal and I had erred somewhere. Maybe the neighbors were right. Twelve children, so many sons, and we had nowhere to go, it seemed. Had we done wrong? But no, we had loved them, we had doted on them, we had taught them right from wrong, we had taught them what we knew . . . yet we went wrong. *Twelve children.*

I let my son escape to his wife and children and didn't mention the visit to Kamal. But I think he knew, for that night as we lay in bed, my back cupped in his chest, he said softly, "Don't mind so much." When I didn't reply he kissed me and drifted off to sleep.

I waited a few days and then talked with our other sons, daughters I could not and would not demean myself by asking for help—the moment they married, they belonged to someone else; they were ours no longer. The boys all came up with some excuse or the other and the final one, when all else failed, was always that it was the eldest son's duty, not theirs. Finally, they came up with a solution. A retirement home.

What was that? I asked in apprehension. And I was right to be frightened of this Western concept that had invaded our existence. Kamal and I moved into this dormitory twenty-three years ago and haven't left it since. The retirement home is too far from the city, so our grandchildren and our children rarely come to visit. All of Kamal's pension goes toward paying the rent here, for two beds in twenty-four. Our children took everything else we possessed. We did not need it here, they said. And so my daughters-in-law and daughters took away my jewels and silver vessels, my sons bullied us until they were allowed to raid our bank account and empty our savings. We had fought, at one time, so long ago, for our country's freedom, but it simply hurt too much to fight for ours. That had been easier.

I watched Kamal age faster than he should have. And God help me, I hated my children. He lost weight, became frail, the veins on his hands stood out green and ugly, his eyes sank into his skull. Physically, he was not the Kamal I knew and loved for so long, but mentally he was as sharp as ever.

And that made our stay here more difficult. After years of building our fortunes and futures and enjoying them both, we were herded around like cattle. Perhaps worse than that.

There was no privacy. We could not talk to each other or walk in the grounds without some orderly lurking in the bushes. The food from the kitchen is not worthy of that name. But more than the physical discomfort, it is the indignity of the whole situation.

It broke Kamal completely. A month ago, he had a heart attack and has been in a coma ever since. He doesn't open his eyes to look at me or say anything. The only sign of life in him is the shallow rise and fall of his rib cage.

Parvati has come back into the room. I look at her kind face and gentle eyes and my heart warms. She has helped me with Kamal, and we owe a lot to this young girl who works here, this child not of our flesh. I wonder sometimes if our daughter—the one who died—would have been like her. The ones who lived are not.

She leans over me. "Shall I turn your head?"

I blink rapidly. Or at least I think I blink; in any case she understands and leaves my head the way it is, on its side, so that I can see Kamal. For four months I stayed in this bed, unable to move after the stroke. One moment everything seemed all right but the next I awoke to a view of the flaky whitewashed ceiling. Kamal was at my side and strangely his eyes were unafraid, full of a smiling courage. There was no way of communicating with him; my throat was frozen up. But he understood me, read to me, talked to me, held my hand (or so he said; I could not feel it).

Our children have not come to visit. Even the news of Kamal's heart attack did not bring them to us. I wonder, briefly, stupidly, if *she* would have come. And I think, to satisfy an old woman's fantasies, that she would have. But none of that matters anymore. Kamal will go soon, I know, and I will follow him. We have not been parted for more than three days at a stretch in all the years we were married.

And there is no reason to do so now.

The Chosen One

*T*his is the only year to which I do not want to return. But I have no choice. As Keeper of the Ten Sins I wander the skies in search of beings with misplaced virtue. The Select Seven, our elders, have established what the sins are—lust, greed, envy, sloth, idiocy, ambition, pride, dishonesty, adulation, and arrogance. I purge our galaxy of these sins. With each obliteration, I grow stronger—and more evil—for the sins come to live in me.

I am a Chosen One.

It is, after all, a coveted job, given to a very few. As a Chosen One, I am knowledgeable—I am, in fact, more intelligent than most, even the Select Seven who chose me. My life as a Chosen One began when I had reached thirty Earth years. There are, in my past, a mate, offspring, even progenitors. All insignificant now. There was also another job; the memory of it is fading, but I see myself as the Gatekeeper, collecting tickets, watching with an inward resentment as crisply dressed travelers are transported to unusual destinations. Destinations I could not afford. Until the Choosing came.

In keeping with the Covenant, I know none of the other Chosen Ones in my circle in their true forms. We do not meet—oh, sometimes in our disguises we do, both in search of the same sin, and when we find it the stronger one wins. I have always won. It is my destiny to do so. Not only am I powerful from absorbing ordinary people, I have in me two other Chosen Ones and their collection of strengths. Sometimes, I think, I seek out the Chosen Ones. Evil is so much easier to garner that way.

It seems simple the way I tell it, but it is not so. When two Chosen Ones collide in the same century, it is because the Select Seven sent us there. And one Chosen One will always end his or her life before the assignment is over. We know *that* but not knowing who is to die makes it better, more exciting. Despite what we do for a living, *to* live, it must be made clear that we do so for the good of the galaxy and its peoples. In current time—my lifetime—many thousands of years have been spent on planet Earth already and mankind has evolved into a degenerate mass, a screaming, pitiful animal. The word *civilization,* indicating civility of any kind, is laughable. The deterioration came slowly, imperceptibly. The only way to correct it is to travel backward and forward in time and annihilate evil using the Chosen Ones.

So, here I stand, in one corner of Asia in a land once

known as India, but now—in travel time—there is no such cohesion in this land. It is a kingdom ruled by a minor king. My voyage watch reads February 1, 1652. That flashes briefly, and then I slip back into my relaxed transition phase and let my thoughts return.

In my heart there has always been a deep, residing hatred, a twisted malice. This is directed toward no special person or thing, it just exists, and it *makes* me exist. It is something I am especially proud of. I am—I have always been—exceptionally suited for this vocation. The Chosen Ones are special, especially to the Select Seven. They watch us carefully, from birth to adulthood, to deem our worthiness before they approach us. And they are the only ones who matter. Well, mattered, anyway.

As I annihilate and my intelligence grows wider than theirs, I find their gentle ways, their soft wisdom, insufferable. They rule with peace and good in mind. Which is why I do what I do; the whole point of my present existence is to destroy evil. Why?

Too often now I find myself torn between wanting that evil in me and admiring it from afar as a thing of extreme and natural beauty. Sometimes, it is almost physically painful to complete an assignment; so much remorse fills me at the loss of a purely evil person to history or to the future. But they, the Select Seven, do not see it as such. With each extinction, history or the future travels a slightly different path—a better route, they say. More and more, I do not agree.

My knowledge grows with each termination, as the evil are often the shrewdest. I take on their characters, their personalities; they die, but live on in me. Then I return to my Chamber of Rest until the urge comes to step out again and let my body travel. I have no control over the time and place I reach. I do not even know, as I arrive, who I am to annihilate. It will all come to me in one sudden moment as I move among these people. In this, the Select Seven have power over me, yes, but it is an inconsequential power. I struggle with the thought that I should control even this aspect. Travel where I want, terminate who I want, or better yet, *not* terminate as I please and allow that evil to blossom. Imagine where we would be now if Dosha had been allowed to possess the minds of all those who inhabited the Earth. When I went in search of her, she could control part of their thoughts already—implant a short dream into their hours of darkness, leave behind confusion when they awoke. She was very close to capturing their waking hours when I absorbed her. It makes me want to cry, if I could cry—Dosha's loss.

Yet for all my bravado, I have always known where I do not want to go. Where a sense of unease plagues me, and this kingdom in 1652 is that one place. In my veins rushes fear, alive and molten. It is such an unusual feeling; it sends a prickly shiver down my spine. But in my head is a flash of excitement. The hunt was getting boring, but no more. No more. There will be danger here, such as I have not tasted since my beginning kills. And if I can overcome this fear, perhaps I will be free to do what I like.

The transition from my world to this one is finally complete, and I look around. During the transition I am aware of where I am going, watching, but not yet fully alert. As it completes, my senses—all those provided by my borrowed body—come to life. It is an alertness that will sustain me through the hazards of the task.

I am standing in the main street of this tiny kingdom in a bazaar of some sort. There is not much activity, a few carts rolling in the dust, their owners muffled in white against the heat and dirt. The shops have long rattan blinds drawn over their fronts. Dogs bark slowly in my direction, their panting tongues dragging in the mud. Ribs show under their blistered skins. The hot, still air is rancid from the stench of a thickly oozing gutter. I lift my head. In the distance, the sun haze wavers over the cool marble dome of a monument, its four minarets punching through the faded blued sky. The minarets have crumpled in present time, my time, the river has engulfed the dome, but on a windless day, when the waters of the river lie tranquil, the submerged dome of the Taj Mahal glows like a pearl. I am not distracted, though; ancient wonders of the world that man has touted as a testament to his meager skill do not interest me.

I look down at myself. The aroma of rose petals rises from my now perspiring skin. I have a sudden vision of being bathed by a female slave this morning. Her touch is soft as she pours warm misting water over me, and then soaps my skin. I can feel the brief, metallic caress of her gold rings. Then comes the massage with an attar of roses. And then the dressing. I am clad in a white silk *dhoti,* wrapped around my waist in neat pleats. My chest is bare and across it lies the sacred thread of the Brahmins. My feet are in leather hide sandals; amulets of gold weigh down my arms.

A small, polite cough is directed at me and I turn to find a shopkeeper standing outside his shop.

"Will you come in, sire?"

I nod and he lifts a cotton blind to let me pass into the cool darkness of the shop. I peer over the low counter to look into a mirror. I like to do this when I travel. My breath hushes at the evenness of my features. No man, not even my original self, was so . . . beautiful. A gleaming, well-oiled crown of hair sits on my head. My eyes are a bright ebony, my lips sensuous, but not enough to be effeminate. There is no question about it; this assignment will be pleasurable. I am what is in these times known as a gentleman of leisure.

When I smile at my image, perfectly chiseled teeth smile back at me, and two dimples deepen my cheeks. Women must find me delightful; I have every intention of being delighted by them. Why not? When I return to my time, all I have energy for is to rest before traveling again. All dalliances must be conducted during my travels; besides, when the time comes the assignment will pull me in. I have little choice in that. Sometimes the assignment will literally claw me from the arms of a beautiful woman in the form of an irate husband who bursts in on us and who is to be annihilated. So I enjoy myself when I can.

"What would you like, sire?" the shopkeeper asks, his head bent in deference.

I know the answer even as he speaks. There is an inner programming that even I am not conscious of, but which guides me to the right responses, which keeps me safe in this whirlwind I live in.

"I hear you have a jewel in your keeping."

"Which one?" he says, gesturing around the dim shop. His cases display ornaments of every kind in gold and silver, sparkling with diamonds, emeralds, garnets, pearls, and rubies. I touch one magnificent necklace, and feel a longing for it. But this is not why I am here.

"A special one," I reply, "with the power to drive a man to madness."

"Ah," he says, nodding, his hands coming together in contemplation. When he looks up, his decision has been made.

"This way, please."

He leads me to a curtain at the back of the shop. We step through it and, leaving the heated street and dingy shop behind, I am transported to another world. We are in a square courtyard belonging to the house behind the shop. Open verandas run along the courtyard leading to various carved wood doors. Two massive mango trees spread their pink spring-flowered branches over the yard. Water gurgles with an afternoon hush into a small pond in the center. A tulasi plant, sweating out its intense fragrance, stands in one corner in a diamond-edged stone pot. I see a few rabbits nibbling on the grass and a doe lifts its head to stare at me with an unblinking, wide gaze.

But all this comes to my subconscious. My conscious mind, my eyes, are drawn to the stone bench under one of the flower-laden mango trees. I draw in a sharp breath through a throat that suddenly chokes. She is, I think painfully in my fast-fogging brain, a jewel that would drive a man mad.

The woman, the goddess in my mind, sits quietly on the bench, the sun dappling her through long mango leaves. On her lap is an earthenware pot and next to her are small jars of paint pigments. I watch, mesmerized, as with a graceful hennaed hand, she dips a brush into one of the jars and with even, sure strokes paints the rim of the pot in intricate circles. The doe wanders near her curiously. She puts out an absentminded hand and it nuzzles her palm. My stomach ties in knots. Lucky doe, I think; what I would not do to lay my face in that palm.

Suddenly, the doe rears away from her, its head whipping around in my direction, and retreats behind the tree. I must have made a sudden movement, but so frozen am I in my thoughts, I do not even realize it. The shopkeeper nudges me slowly and I turn to him in a trance. He stretches out his hand in an age-old gesture of want. I now feel the weight of the chamois bag tied around my waist, hanging heavy against my thigh. Without looking at him, I find the knot and untie the bag. It is his without counting, for money—this money—is worthless to me anyway, and for her nothing can be too much. I barely notice him depart as I descend the stone steps into the courtyard. She looks up at me then.

"Hush," she says, her voice sending excruciating goose bumps up my arm. "No slippers, please."

I obey, slipping off my sandals, that voice still echoing in my numbed ears. How did she know I was coming?

She beckons and that thought is forgotten. I move toward her. On the stone pathway, pebbles bite into the soles of my feet; in the grass, I sink ankle-deep and dewy blades whisper against my skin. The doe, hiding behind the tree, her nostrils quivering in fright, flees on elegant legs. The rabbits leap behind a stone and stand there, their fur on edge. I always have this effect on animals. It is the only glitch the programming has, and many a time has almost revealed us Chosen Ones as unusual beings in whatever time we travel to.

But the woman does not notice, and I continue to approach her. Her image is to me a jumble of impressions. The skin is poured cream. Her eyelashes fan down over liquid eyes. Her eyebrows arch like the wings of a dove. Her hair is a color the midnight sky would envy, blue-black and straight, shimmering to below the end of her spine. Her tiny waist, the heave of her breasts, the smell of snowy jasmines threaded in a garland around her neck—all make me quicken my step.

When I sit down next to her, a wave of nausea hits my body. When it passes, I look up in wonder. Her effect on me is so strong, I am almost physically sick. I had not wanted to travel to this assignment, but it was showing signs of being the best voyage yet.

She takes my hand in hers; her palm is cool and soft in my now-perspiring one. Her thumb rolls slowly over my skin. A dull throb starts at the base of my neck as I lean into her hand and kiss the fingers. The fragrance of sandalwood oil fills my nostrils and starts the edge of a headache. She pulls my hand again and lets it rest on the earthenware pot on her lap.

"Feel this," she says softly. The pot feels cool and damp against my skin and I take a deep breath to dispel the pain between my eyebrows.

"It is a music pot," she says. "I paint and sell them to musicians. Listen."

She raps the pot lightly with her left hand and a sweet, hollow tone rings out, reverberating around the silent courtyard. I suddenly realize how silent it is. There are no birds in the trees, a quietness lies over us, even the water flowing to the pond has dried up. The throb at the bottom of my neck deepens and I groan. I cannot be falling sick, this body cannot be falling sick already. Only twice before, during my voyages, have I sensed these aches and pains in my altered state. And both were . . .

The agony in my head intensifies, spreading down over my shoulders into my whole body. She is still holding my hand, an amused look on her face. My energy seems to be draining into her. I try to pull back but I cannot, there is little strength left. I realize then. The other two times were during meetings with other Chosen Ones, the ones who are in me, the ones I killed. The termination of ordinary mortals is never this painful, and if I had not been swept away by her beauty I would have realized it before. Touching another Chosen One willingly, as I have done, is an invitation to death; my power has been sapped without my knowledge. And thus have I before executed my Chosen Ones.

I struggle now, furiously and fast, but she holds me tight. She has the advantage, I did not see her, did not know her. How could that be? How was it the Select Seven sent me here to be annihilated and I had no inkling of what was to come? And I know why. I made the mistake of thinking myself more powerful than them. How was I so stupid all of a sudden? I knew they were tapped into my consciousness all the time, how could I have thought such thoughts and allowed them to see my revulsion? And yet how could I not think? Too late, too late, my shrinking brain tells me. I had learned from the Select Seven that ultimate strength came not from brute might, but from the ability to read a mind in its entirety. I knew that well, also from Dosha who had resided in me so long . . . now she was fleeing to this other Chosen One. I had, in these final moments of my existence, added idiocy to my list of sins. The irony would have made me laugh—if I could have laughed then.

The struggle is too hard, I feel my feet turn leaden, my torso empties as she reaches down my throat to grab my stomach, more excruciating is the drain of evil, and the drain of knowledge from my brain. I fight, I kick mentally, and now, too late again, I see the light of the Chosen One be-hind her eyes. The animals ran, I think thickly, from her at first then from the combined evil in both of us. If only I had seen it earlier . . . A red blindness comes over me as my head explodes.

I am in her and I watch my borrowed body turn blue, green, then into a brief miasma of my early Earth self, and then it disappears. She, my Chosen One host, sighs and picks up the brush to paint her pot. As she does so, she forces me to go over my last voyage again, from the moment I find myself on the bazaar street, knowing I fear this voy-age, not knowing why, but also feeling that deceptive sense of excitement.

Hunger

I meet Sheela a month after load shedding begins for the summer. March in Mumbai—temperatures ascend steadily and the air is dry and tangy with exhaust fumes. Skies plead for clouds, air conditioners cough and hum, and electric lines fry from an overload of use. At least two more blinding months before the monsoons. This summer the public works department decides to shut down the city (known by the unlovely appellation of load shedding) for four hours every day, eleven to three in the afternoon, and everything—companies, industries, Bollywood film sets—slows to a *nimbupani* and ganna juice–sipping, tandoori chicken–eating, sweat-swiping, cigarette-smoking torpor. The taxi drops me off in front of our building and even before I go in I know there is a long climb ahead. Munshi, our watchman, sits chewing *paan* on the front parapet under the gulmohur tree, legs splayed.

"No light, memsahib," he says, scratching under his khaki shirt.

I stand in front of him, my arms spilling with the shopping. He does not offer to help and I do not ask. Munshi always wants too much of a tip. For what? The building association pays his salary—far more generous than the one I get. Which is nothing. And I do a lot more work than Munshi, who seems to spend all his time on the parapet, whistling slyly after the giggling maids. I tell Prakrit that we should sack Munshi and I will do his job instead. How hard can it be to lift a hand in a halfhearted salute when the managing director passes, or ogle at the new wives in the building, or ignore visitors when they ask questions?

Prakrit, being Prakrit, is properly horrified at my suggestion. "Nitu, you are my *wife*," he hisses. "What would the MD think? What would people think?"

Munshi grins again with barely concealed satisfaction. His face is smooth, like a much-used mortar stone, brown like dirt. "Fourteen floors, memsahib," he says, holding up ten fingers and then four.

"I know where I live, Munshi." I go into the cool darkness of the building, sweeping as majestically as I can past Munshi's smirk, and confront the lifeless lifts. If I leave my bags in the little cupboard in the lobby and return for them when the electricity comes back, half their contents will have disappeared. The lifts gape back at me, their faces painted a mocking, hospital green. Munshi's color choice. The association voted for blue, but for the budget we had, Munshi got us green . . . cheap, very cheap, memsahib.

As I stand there, someone else comes in. The light is behind her and for a moment I cannot see her face, only a thin figure clad in jeans and a loose T-shirt that hangs in the still air. I look away as she approaches, it would be rude to stare, but strangely she comes up to me and smiles.

"Hello."

I turn in surprise. People rarely talk to one another in our building, we just bestow on-the-edge-of-civil pleasantries as we take the lift or meet in the lobby. Unless the woman you are trying to ignore is your husband's manager's wife, then you smile very much at her until she ignores you. This is the way building hierarchy works. Of course, the company does not own the entire building, just fifty flats. But I can tell civilians from company workers. Was this girl one of Prakrit's juniors' wives?

I turn away from her with a cardboard smile, playing my part as best I can. Prakrit is not very senior yet, but one day he will be, and I need to learn how to do this.

"It looks like the electricity is off, but this is not the right time for it to go, is it?" she says.

"No," I reply, despite myself. "Today it has gone off much earlier." Now I see her properly. Her face is as though unfinished, no lipstick, and her hair is pulled back in a ponytail. She must be someone's daughter; no wife can be so young nowadays. They all seem to wait, to finish their degrees, to get jobs, to have children. They wait with a voice I did not have; now I will never have it.

"Fourteen floors is a long way, can I help?" She starts pulling packages from my arms without waiting for a reply.

"How do you know?"

"Oh, I know who you are. I've seen you before with your children. They are beautiful, like little gods. Such perfect, unspoiled faces. Like yours a little."

I look at her, mute. So much praise. I am suspicious. Who is this girl? What does she want? As I try to wrestle my belongings from her, she waves me away and says, "We are in 8A. Jai, my husband, he works with your husband, same department. Our flat faces the slums, terrible view, but what interesting and smelly lives they lead, always fighting, always screaming at each other, but at eight o'clock when *Rishta* comes on Channel 5, everything stops. Jai and I watch them when we have nothing else to do."

Eighth floor. Definitely Prakrit's junior, although the way she says it, it seems like they work together in the same position. But the higher you live, the more senior you are in the company. Eight is almost half of fourteen. I must not be too familiar, but gracious.

"Coming?"

She has the door to the stairs propped open with one Keds-clad foot, her hip holding it in place. I nod and follow her through, trying to be distant. After so many years of wearing a sari, I have still not mastered the art of climbing stairs gracefully in one. *Kick your pleats as you walk, keep your back straight, head high,* not one lesson sticks. Prakrit always says I lumber in a sari, no grace, stick to *salwars,* Nitu. I plod ahead of the girl, one hand holding my pleats up from the ground. I can hear her skipping up the steps behind me. Even when I was her age, I did not skip; girls were in training to be ladies. I stop at the first landing, already out of breath. Fourteen landings loom in front of me, this girl will leave at eight, how will I go up the rest alone?

"I will come up to your floor," she says. "Jai tells me the view is fabulous from your flat."

"Jai has been to our home?"

"Yes, a few months ago, right after we were married, before I came to Mumbai. My Bapa did not want me to leave home so soon after the wedding; he convinced Jai to let me stay for three weeks saying I had to get my completion certificate from college." She laughs, a trilling, youthful sound. It makes her face glow. "I need the certificate to get a job here, only Jai does not want me to work, not yet anyway. He thinks we should start a family first. But this morning I went for an interview at an advertising firm. They offered me a job."

So candid, so much information in just a few minutes of knowing her. This is the new way. In my day, we did not talk so much or so openly. And that too about having children with those smiles—we blushed when we talked of children for they came through, well, you know, the way they come.

"When did Jai come to our home?" I ask again.

"Let me see . . ." Her well-sculpted eyebrows meet in thought as we climb the stairs again. Thankfully, I am not talking anymore. But her voice goes on. "July, no August. No, no, it was July. We were married in May; Jai came back here almost immediately. I followed in July." Again that laugh, white teeth shining. "I guess I stayed back home with Bapa longer than a few weeks." A wink now. "My college is very backward in giving out certificates, then I had to get my marks sheets also."

"Jai did not mind?"

"Oh, I think he minded. But Bapa can be very strong when he wants. I don't have a mother; she died when I was two. Bapa brought me up alone, did not marry again, he thought the new wife might be cruel to me. Sometimes, though, I wish he had, it would have been nice to have a mother. Like when I got my period. At first, I simply could not go to Bapa and ask him to buy me sanitary napkins."

"What did you do?" I ask, interested despite myself. A single man bringing up a girl child on his own. People must have talked. And so unusual to not want a wife who would take care of the child.

"I thought of going to the neighbor auntie's house, but she and Bapa always squabbled over something or the other. She would tell him not to let me wear jeans, unwomanly she would say. The next day I had five new jeans and I wore them each day until she fought with Bapa again. There was no one else around. The neighbor auntie only had boys, I could not ask them. In the end, I asked Bapa."

I am horrified and stop on the stairs, panting a little. But the curiosity again. "What did your Bapa do?"

"He sat me down on the drawing room sofa and drew a picture of a uterus, the ovaries, and explained how an egg was released and what a period was. Then, he went to the nearby pharmacy and came back with a newspaper-wrapped package. I read the instructions on the cover and did the rest myself. For the next few months Bapa bought me the napkins; then I started to buy them. It was horrible how the shop boys grinned at me. What a fuss about something normal."

"Poor thing," I say.

We stop on another landing, number six. Here too the walls are painted green and white, smudged at shoulder level. There is a staggering smell of old urine rising from the floor, and crushed *beedi* stubs are everywhere.

The girl sniffs, wrinkling a broad nose. She wears a diamond nose stud. For all her talk, she is old-fashioned enough to wear a nose stud. "Bathroom."

"What?" I manage between heaves of piss-filled air.

"This was the bathroom," she says. "See, the chap leaned his hands on the wall here." She points. "He urinated here. Gross. Let's go."

We move on, almost running up the stairs this time. She has her face buried in the plastic bag from the Sari Emporium. "Gross," she says again.

The only gross I know is a measure of weight.

"Do you remember the man who lived on the landings? Fourth landing sleeping area. Fifth the kitchen. Sixth was the bathroom. Until Munshi found him and kicked him out."

"He was Munshi's brother," I say, panting.

"Really?" She turns *kajal*-rimmed eyes at me. She has a classic face. Big eyes, thick lashes, big nose but a nice big nose, lips that pout. Even her body is an Indian man's dream. Lushly rounded with a span-with-two-hands waist, like the carved stone maidens adorning temple walls. Completely unsuited to jeans and a T-shirt. She should be clad in an almost-transparent chiffon sari with a backless blouse. "How do you know?"

"Munshi let him stay in the landings, until the load shedding started and people started taking the stairs. The MD came home one day for lunch, unexpectedly, and found the man asleep on the landing. It was then Munshi pretended to have suddenly discovered he was living here."

"The bastard." She says this casually. When I was growing up, I could not even say *bloody*. She must be only fifteen years younger than me, around twenty-five or so, yet she seems so wise, so confident.

By the time we reach the fourteenth floor, I am exhausted. The plastic bags slip from my sweating hands. As I fumble with the keys, she looks out of the landing window. I drag myself into the flat and sit on the drawing room sofa. I did not leave the windows open, the cool of the air conditioner has long since evaporated, and the room is stifling. She unlatches the windows and stands there, heat blasting through the grill, borne on an undercurrent of sweet air. That betraying hint of the monsoons, mocking and not to come for many months yet.

"Can I have some water please?"

"Of course." I start to rise.

"No, no. Tell me where. I will go get it."

I point to the kitchen and listen as she finds two steel tumblers and fills them with ice water from a jug in the fridge.

"Thank you for helping me with the bags."

She sits next to me on the sofa and fingers the parcels. "You went to buy saris?"

"Yes, for the party."

"Which party?"

"At the MD's house. Oh, you are not invited?"

A laugh scurries over her face. "No, not yet. Jai is too junior, you know, to be asked for dinner at the managing director's flat. One day he will get promoted and then I will have to be stolid and sulky like the other managers' wives."

I never dared to talk like this, with such disrespect. "The children will be coming from school. I have to make them something to eat."

She gets up and stretches. Her arms are long, reaching mid-thigh when she lets them down. "I have to go plan dinner. Jai wants a full dinner every night. *Chappatis,* rice, a *dal,* a *subji,* and a dessert. I tease him that he did not marry a cook but a wife. No use, you know."

"Was yours an arranged marriage?" The words slip out without my realizing. I flush. I was becoming a manager's wife, asking the same prying questions I had been asked when I first came here.

She turns, hands on her hips. "Yes. The neighbor auntie pestered my Bapa until he agreed to let Jai come to see me.

She is his aunt, his mother's cousin. The auntie thought that since I had reached womanhood it was unseemly to let me live alone with my father." She wrinkles her nose and lines pepper her forehead. "How ugly people can get."

"She is right, you know," I say gently. This girl is a child, with a child's naivete, a child's supreme and misplaced confidence.

"I don't love Jai."

Shock tears over me at those words.

"Well"—her mouth twists—"I *like* him, but I don't love him, not like all those women in the Mills & Boon romances. I thought it would be the same as living with my Bapa. Just substitute one man for another. But it is not the same, not worse, but different."

I am still appalled. Again, something I will never dare to say. Prakrit is my life. He is supposed to be; he is my husband, my *patidev,* my husband-who-is-akin-to-God. I will not say in public, or even think in private, that I do not revere and respect him. My mother teaches me this. Now I know why this girl does not know how to talk about Jai—because she has no mother.

She comes up and stands in front of me, one eyebrow raised. It arcs over her forehead like a perfect rainbow. I like this quizzical look in this woman-child. She slants her head over one shoulder, then another. My panting has ceased now, and an errant breeze washes over us from the grill-clad window. I am sunk into the sofa's cushions, my stomach folded over the petticoat of my sari. I pull the *pallu* to hide it. She reaches to my head with a long-fingered hand, nails painted pearl silver. When I flinch she says, "Wait."

She pulls the rubber band from my hair and it splays over my shoulders. I feel decadent, sitting there with my hair out. It is not Sunday, the only day I wash and let my hair loose. "What lovely hair you have, so thick, do you use *amla* oil?"

"Yes. And coconut, both mixed. And henna sometimes."

"Ah, I see the red highlights now."

She has switched topics with such ease, blocking out what she said a few minutes ago. I do not love Jai. Just like that. Unrepentant. Unaware of having revealed something deep and secret.

She leaves soon after with a wave. She says something as she goes, why don't you trim your hair of split ends. Split ends. An end that is split.

So many years ago now. Fourteen? Fifteen? At first the news that the broker, Auntie Agha, has many many prospects. Then the excitement when she comes, heaving her body into the best chair in the room as my father looks on disapprovingly. But Agha is indifferent, isn't she bringing the best prospect of them all and doesn't it deserve the rattan chair at the head of the room? I hear words as I pass by. America. Good job. Makes a lot of money. How much? my mother asks suspiciously—other much-money-makers have turned out to be clerks in banks. A lot, Agha says firmly. In dollars, that too. Mother deflates at that word; her daughter, if she is lucky, will live with dollars. Did he study in America? No, no, but no matter, eh? Well . . . Mother is doubtful, she looks at my father, who is slightly mollified at the mention of America, but still thunderous at the loss of his chair. My mother sees me at the door and shoos me away. When we want you to know about the man you are to marry you will know, as much as we decide to tell you. This is not any of your business right now. They set a date for Prakrit to come to the house.

The next day he surprises me at the law firm where I work.

The law secretary, an ancient man in black-rimmed Gandhi glasses stops at my desk and snipes, distaste tinge-ing his words, "A man to see you. Your brother?" He knows I have no brother. I glare at him. Why shatter my reputa-tion when I don't even know what I have done? The visitor floods our little whitewashed office with its grimy windows and floors with his aftershave.

"Nitu?" The voice is smooth, an accent, not unpleasant, when he says *Neetoo*. "I'm Prakrit."

All at once I am spiraling into confusion, aware I don't smell nice (no deodorant and the talcum powder has long burned off), or look presentable (sweat-matted hair glued to my neck), wear a frowning forehead (the law secretary has been yelling at me all morning), and sit hunched (trying to hide the folds of my stomach where my blouse gapes at the waist). He looks nice and pale, as though America kills color in the skin, and cool as though still under a weak American sun.

American-fashion, he puts out his hand. I give him a

weak one, fingertips only, and he waggles them. "I thought we should meet under less formal circumstances. Much easier this way, no aunties and mothers watching." He laughs and I watch his teeth in fascination. I don't say anything.

"Anyhow," he continues, "this whole arranged marriage thing is so boring, so outdated. As though you were a horse for sale."

Admiration fills me. I am still dumb, wondering now if I have rubbed the *kajal* from my eyes onto my cheeks in black streaks, powerless to wipe with a furtive finger and find out. Prakrit is my number seven. The previous six alliances all rejected me as I paraded in front of them and they checked my weight, and height, and skin color, and teeth, and my other less visible assets. They would say things like, "My dearest dream is to see my daughter-in-law on the *mandap,* clad in an auspicious red sari, glittering with jewels—how many *tolas* of gold will you be putting on her, by the way?" Or "My son takes the bus to work every day and comes home so, so tired he can barely talk, all that pushing and shoving to get inside, those servants and tradesmen with their baskets—a scooter, or better yet a car would be nice for him." Or "We want a daughter who will work; one income is so little nowadays. But I plan to put my feet up and let her take charge of the house and the servants. I will give her the keys to the storeroom and she can cook and make sure the vessels are washed and the clothes are folded—tell me, how much income does your daughter make?"

My response to all of these questions is always None of

your business and they take off offended. One "boy" even grabs a *pakora* on his way out, stuffing his mouth with it and saying, "No one will want to marry such a modern girl, teach her better manners, or else." And that "or else" hangs over my parents' heads as they optimistically groom me and brush my hair and teeth and teach me to neigh at the right places. How does Prakrit know all this?

"So do you have a voice? If so, I would like to heere it."

I fall in love with the way he says *hear.*

"I think so too," I say, answering his comment on arranged marriages being boring and old-fashioned. I have never been anything but bored. Until now.

His eyebrows are thick and they rise into even thicker hair on his head. "You are fifth on my list."

He has gone through four already? There is no way I will pass the test. "What was wrong with them?" My voice squeaks. I stand abruptly and knock a few law books off the table. He bends to pick them up.

"Shall I sit?"

"Please . . ." I rush around the side and force him into my chair, and pull another one up. The ceiling fan clanks alarmingly, it does this every few hours and I always watch to see if it is going to fall. "Chai, er, do you want some tea? *Pakoras?*"

My hands are damp and trembling. I yell at the peon. "Shekar, go get some tea and biscuits from the chai shop, and don't put your fingers in the cup."

"Please, allow me." Prakrit stands up, reaches for his

wallet, and pulls out two crisp ten-rupee notes. He hands them to a gawking Shekar. "Keep the change."

I translate that unique order to Shekar and he salaams four times as he backs out of the room, still agawk.

"It's too much. The chai is only three rupees."

Prakrit waves grandly, bringing a rush of some manly perfume, all dulled edges and no scent of flowers, into the air around me. "Sit. Let me talk to you, Neetoo."

My heart thumps wildly; all of a sudden I want this man who with such flourish throws money at peons. How does one dollar translate into rupees? Forty rupees to a dollar? Something like that, but still such élan. Does he do this in America too? Cast away twenty rupees worth without so much as a thought? Like a film star.

"So are you a law secretary?" he asks, taking out a red-and-white pack of Marlboros. "Cigarette?"

I shake my head. Is he joking? Is this a test? What good Indian girl smokes—well, in public anyway?

He lights it with a silver lighter and blows smoke at the ceiling fan. It shudders in response.

"Just a secretary," I manage, still watching the smoke swirl around the small office. "Didn't Auntie Agha tell you that?"

"Ah, the inimitable Agha, with her reams of girls all waiting to marry me. She says to me the day after I arrive in India, What do you want, Prakrit? A doctor? A lawyer? An IIM graduate? An IIT graduate? Should she sing? Dance Odissi or Bharatanatyam? How many brothers and sisters should she have? Too many, too little?"

My head sinks as I hear him. So much choice. And among all these girls surely there is one who will fit perfectly. Skin creamy as milk, eyelashes shadowing a seductive glance, a brain trained at the best engineering college, hands that will cook dishes worthy of a five-star hotel's kitchen, and a uterus capable of bearing many sons. Why me? Is he here just to mock this plain secretary, six times dumped already?

"But," he continues, "I say I want a girl who I can talk with. Just that. Someone who is not so full of herself. A companion, who will fill my hours in the United States with fun."

My head snaps up. "Tell me about yourself, Prakrit."

He smiles. I think the room lights up, suddenly not so dingy anymore. I push one of the law books under the growing ash on his cigarette and admire the way he taps the end and a long worm of gray reposes on the dull pages. Later, after he leaves, I tip the ashes carefully into an envelope emblazoned with the name of the firm. The law secretary complains about the loss of stationery when I leave my job; he keeps close tabs on every sheet of paper in the office.

That evening when Prakrit comes home I tell him about Jai's wife. She did not tell me her name, and I forgot to ask.

"Ah, Jai from the eighth floor. Mr. Up-and-Coming. The bright, blue-eyed boy of the company."

"He has blue eyes?" I ask, ignoring the rest of Prakrit's statement.

"Figure of speech, Nitu. Don't act too smart, you're not."

He throws down his executive briefcase that the latest promotion allows him to carry. Picking up a samosa, he bites into it. I watch him anxiously; does he notice how perfect it has turned out, taste the new *garam masala* I ground myself? I bring him chai. It has been many years since he has said, honey, I'm home, when he comes through the door with his still-left-over-from-America twang. His face is shuttered as he sits at the table, unyielding. Sunny and Dinesh are in their bedrooms. Homework time. Only when they are finished can they come to say hello to Daddy.

Prakrit eats two more samosas and drinks his chai without a word. I sit across from him at the table, with an expectant understanding expression. The same one my mother wears every day when my father comes home from work. Early on, Prakrit used to find this hilarious. Come off it, Neetoo, you don't have to wait on me hand and foot, like some godforsaken ancient woman of old. I'm not that kind of a husband.

My mother scolds me when I agree with him. Your husband is a *devta,* Nitu, a god. Your god. Do you press his feet every night? Do you touch his feet with reverence in the morning? Touch your forehead to his feet?

I try this for the first few mornings as Prakrit still sleeps (I am to wake earlier than him, that is the rule), but one morning he moves suddenly and slams me against the side of the cot. Blood everywhere from a cut above my eye, blinding me, and Prakrit yells. Something about weird traditions. For pity's sake, Neetoo.

That was fifteen years ago.

I wait for him to talk. He burps loudly and rubs his cheek. The impending shadow of a beard lies heavy on his face; he has to shave at least twice a day. Now he wears a mustache like the other men in the company. I hate it, it's like kissing a broom, but then I have not kissed him in many years.

"What happened?"

"Mehta from accounting got promoted to manager today," he says.

"Double-chin Mehta? Why? He's just started working at the company."

"His wife made Diwali sweets for the MD. *Laddus* and *jalebis, kaju barfis* and *petas*. He says she made them. But he got them from Shantiram's, as I did."

I am consoling. "Next Diwali I will make the sweets myself for the MD."

He laughs, the beard shadow spreading black across his face. "How, Nitu? You can't even cook."

"I made the samosas and the chai."

"Any idiot can make samosas."

Any idiot can't. Knead the *maida* just right, roll it out, cut into semicircles, stuff with potatoes and peas, fashion into three-dimensional, mountain-shaped pieces. Fry in Dalda until golden brown and crisp. Drain. It is true though that I do not cook the dinner or the lunch, the *bai* does. Among the other maidenly things my mother teaches me, cooking is not one I grasp with flourish. I have tried, since we first married I have tried. But Prakrit, his palate refined in American restaurants, cannot stomach my efforts. Sunny and Dinesh can—thank God they have dull tongues.

"Did Sunny pass her Maths test?"

I am dreading this question. "No. But just two marks less than pass. It is all right, she will do better next time, Prakrit."

He turns to the bedrooms. "Sunny, come here!"

"Prakrit." I grab his sleeve. "Let her be. She is upset. She—"

"Sunny!"

She comes and stands at the edge of the corridor, her new jeans already cut off at pedal-pusher length, frayed and slaughtered. She's falling headlong into womanhood, this child of mine. Her breasts are beginning to show against her T-shirt at just eleven. We have been fighting about the bra I will not buy her. Why not, all my friends wear one. Not until, I say. Until what, I get my chums, is that it? I turn away horrified, talking about . . . well, about . . . that thing even before she has it. When I became a woman, my mother in a very businesslike fashion gave me a strip of cloth until the servant brought sanitary napkins from the store. The rest I learned from my friends amid giggles and complaints of cramps and stories of eight days of bleeding.

Sunny is chewing bubble gum, blowing bubbles in thick pink circles, and then peeling them with a magenta-painted fingernail from her nose and mouth. Her T-shirt gapes at her stomach.

"What the hell are you doing dressed like that?" Prakrit is really angry now, red flushes on his neck. When did that neck grow fat?

"Like what, Daddy?" Another chew and cheeks puffed to blow.

"Throw away that disgusting stuff. Where is your respect for your elders? Why didn't you pass your Maths exam?"

"Saroj Miss does not like me, that's why." She leans against the wall on one skinny hip (how thin she is) and folds her arms across her chest.

They fight, back and forth. Prakrit demanding respect, Sunny stubbornly refusing to give it. Eventually, Sunny's face crumples into tears and she turns and runs back to the bedroom.

Prakrit slouches, muttering to himself, as he loosens the tie from his grime-rimmed collar with a thick finger. Once he lets me do this for him, watching my hands tug at the knot, slipsliding the tie from his neck. He is full of smiles, bending to bite my fingers, all this even after the children are born. Once.

A blast of music deafens the flat as Dinesh opens his bedroom door.

"Hi, Daddy. My homework is done." He comes to us carrying a miniature silver cup. "Elocution at school. First prize." He's like Prakrit, more like him than Sunny. Dinesh has his father's squat figure, the heavy brows, that sun-bright smile. But as much as Prakrit tries to teach him what it is to be a man, Dinesh is still more mine than his. That will never change. Now Dinesh comes to be petted and patted. We both praise him; I've seen the cup three times already, once when he waved it under Sunny's just-failed-Maths nose. Then Sunny glared at him and marched off, and Dinesh ran to his room to get her the comic book they have been fighting over. Without my telling him.

When Dinesh leaves, Prakrit rises to go to the bedroom and says over his shoulder, "Get the *bai* to come in for the night. We are going to The Tapping Foot at ten o'clock."

"Prakrit!" I run after him but he is already in the bathroom, his shoes kicked off at the door, his socks on the floor, his tie, his shirt (redolent of him) and his pants on the bed.

He switches on the water heater and starts to lather his chin.

"A disc? We are going to a disc at our age?"

He looks at me in the mirror. "All the managers are going with their wives. The MD wants to see me there. Wear something nice. Not Indian. Western." He bends down again.

I am still standing at the door when he shuts it. I turn away in slow steps. First the *bai*.

Munshi is sleeping on the parapet in front of the building when I come out of the lift, his Nehru cap over his eyes. He does not even raise it as he says, "*Bai* taken already, memsahib. By 15A, memsahib."

"Get up, Munshi. Get up and stand when you talk to me."

He bolts upright, the venom in my voice frightening him. But soon that slow, insolent smile. "*Bai* will not come to your flat tonight, memsahib."

"We'll see." I walk around the compound wall and down the little mound of dirt into the slum where our *bai* lives. She sees me coming but continues to chop a cauliflower, her latest child suckling at her breast. She's barely respectful in the flat, working for me, now even less so. As I near she spits out a red streak of *paan* on the ground next to her. A TV blares inside her shack and her three older children sit on the floor, eyes pinned to the color screen. A satellite dish (do I pay her that much?) pokes out of the thatched roof.

"*Bai,* the sahib and I are going out tonight. I need you to come and look after the children."

"Not possible, memsahib. I have to take care of my children."

"*Bai,* please. Just this one time."

She unlatches the baby from her breast, tucks it under her blouse, swings him around, and pulls out the other breast. I look away. When she first has this child, I do not allow her to bring him into the flat while she works, for she stops often to feed his cries. Dinesh and Sunny halt whatever they are doing, which is usually lounging on the sofa gorging themselves on comics, and gape at that brown nipple. She thinks I am cruel, but I am just practical. I don't want my children, then perhaps my husband, looking at another woman's breast, even if she is only a *bai*.

We go back and forth in that slum, as the other servants come out to stare at me, pricing my gold bangles, my *mangalsutra,* my diamond earrings, and my Bata sandals from their shack doors. The *bai* settles eventually for two hundred rupees and two Sundays off. I wonder how much the 15A memsahib promised the *bai*. They live one floor above us, but the memsahib is cheap. Obviously.

The disc is on the ground floor of the Maha Taj hotel. It reeks of an opulence that makes my skin cold. Heavy glass doors. A gold-and-red-brocade-clad doorman with upturned Jodhpur slippers on his feet and a plumed gold *zari* turban on his head. Like a bridegroom or a decked-out horse. He opens the door for us with one hand, the other clasps Prakrit's hand as a fifty-rupee note passes between them. First Munshi, now this man. I should be doing this job. How hard can it be to heave a well-oiled door open and look stupidly magnificent? We pass into the frigid marble-floored lobby. The receptionists lounge over polished granite counters, dulcet-voiced, dutifully ignoring us. Five-star hotels don't have five-star receptions for less-than-managing-director types like us.

"Prakrit." I hold on to the sleeve of his cotton shirt. He looks clean after his bath, like the man who came to see me all those years ago at the law office. Today he uses the last of his American cologne and the smell sticks around me. "Let's go home."

"Don't be silly, Nitu." He peels my fingers away and holds me at a distance. Early on he would touch me often, bringing red flushes of embarrassment over my skin. In public, that is. In front of my mother and father who looked away disapprovingly. In front of his parents who smirked at the evidence that their son was having sex. This is what touching in public means, sex, not affection. This is why I blush. I know this too.

"We have to go in. You look fine. Don't worry."

I am wearing pants and a halter shirt. Prakrit does not let me wear a sari or a *salwar,* too Indian, not Western enough, we're going to a disc for God's sake, Nitu, not a temple. Dress appropriately.

I haven't worn this shirt in many years; I think my breasts are too heavy, bulging over the front. I adjust the straps and slink into the disc behind Prakrit. Noise blasts out at us, drowning everything.

"Over there!" Prakrit yells in my ear, and I feel my eardrum reverberate painfully.

Strobe lights in blue, green, red, and purple puncture the darkened room. A silver ball glitters in the center of the ceiling. The music, cacophonous, is a thud of techno-funk. *Boom. Boom. Boom.* Over and over again. No other rhythm, no voices, no singing. Just a guitar and a heavy set of drums. We cleave through wedges of people; I see Prakrit's back appear and disappear.

Someone puts a thick arm across my front and says, "Wanna dance, baby?"

America has come to India now, thank you, MTV. Sunny and Dinesh, unprompted, will say Mom I am ass-king you. I still say aahsk, not ass. When I aahsk them what ass is, they are all giggles and Mom you are *so* old.

I turn to look at the hairless-faced boy. "Are you mad?" I yell into his ear. "You're young enough to be my son."

He mouths, I like mamas.

"Nitu." Prakrit grabs my hand. The boy frames a V with his fingers—peace, man, didn't mean to hit on your old lady. Prakrit drags me away and I stumble on my spiked heels. Everyone in the disc is years younger. Their faces are vapid, drug-hazed, their arms and legs flail, hair flies about their shoulders. The girls wear too much skin and too little clothing.

The others are waiting for us in a dim alcove. Glasses litter the table, some rimmed with half-lips in lipstick. The MD sits in the middle of the semicircular booth, his wife on one side, his secretary, all pale skin and strappy dress, on the other side.

"This is the youth of today, Prakrit," he bawls, his smooth domed head glittering in the fast-moving light of the room. "From here will come the future of the company."

From these children who dance with such abandon, who are so deafened by the sound that they do not need to think, just act. The MD has already had too many drinks. His wife looks furious as his hand brushes the secretary's thigh, as his bleary eyes rest too long on the scooped neckline of her silver lamé dress.

We sit and Prakrit mimes two gin and tonics to the waiter. It is what the MD is drinking. I hate gin—water with a kick. A taste of metal. I want wine, but I drink gin.

My head gets slowly accustomed to the roar of music, my eyes still reel from the flash of colors, but if I look into my drink, it is not so bad. Everyone is watching the children on the dance floor. In a few years, Sunny and Dinesh will be here. *Boom. Boom. Boom.* Moving to a rhythm that makes no sense to me, Prakrit's old lady. I see the others from the company to one side of the floor. They are all shuffling, dutifully twitching shoulders, one even does a John Travolta stance, pelvis kicked out, one arm bent, the other high in the air. The children who see him giggle. They get closer to one another, hips moving in mimicry of sex, the boys' eyes lustful and vague, as though in the throes of passion. There is a hunger in them. A bare-naked hunger on the edge of starvation. It is so stark, it is embarrassing. A hunger that makes them forget etiquette and rules, and in doing so, makes them mesmerizing to me. They laugh at the company people. Mehta from accounting, who just got promoted, stomps his feet, his diminutive Diwali-sweets-making wife stomps faithfully along with him, ill-at-ease and poured into a green silk jumpsuit that barely contains her.

"Go! Go, dance!" the MD shouts, patting Prakrit on the back.

Just then a hand touches my neck. I turn to see the girl. Her T-shirt is black this time, off the shoulders, her waist bare. She has a ring in her navel. "Hi."

"Prakrit, this is—"

But he is rising already, and almost overturns his G&T. Looking very manly. He shakes her hand and I hear her say, "Sheela, Jai's wife."

"Do you want to dance, Sheela?" he yells.

"Yes, but with your wife. Come." She pulls me up.

I shake my head with a fury. "No. No. No. You two go. I will watch."

"No fun that way. Come."

We fight our way to the floor. The music is louder now, harsher. I am still shaking my head and she is laughing. "You're not that old, you know."

In the skittering light I watch her as I shift my weight from one foot to another. She is wearing a black chiffon skirt that swirls around her, an armlet of glittering stone on one naked arm. When she lifts her hands to clap I see clean armpits without even a shadow of hair. She has gold eyeshadow on, and little sparkles of metal in her foundation that catch the light as she turns her face. I watch her.

She leans over and says, "Come to the bathroom."

We melt into the crowd to the bathroom in one corner. We piss. We don't talk. When I come out, she is waiting, leaning against the sink. I wash my hands, thinking, She doesn't love Jai. She doesn't love Jai. Somehow that thought shatters me. When I reach for the towel, she takes it from me and wipes my hands carefully as I have done for Sunny and Dinesh when they are younger. As I still sometimes do. But her touch is nothing like mine, nothing that is motherly. When she is done, she continues to hold my hands. I want this. I want this with a hunger I did not know I had.

I am crying now, looking down at my hands and crying with tears that do not seem to stop. Sheela leans over and licks the tears from my face, slowly, without fear. I wait. I watch her. She kisses me on the mouth. A gentle kiss. Of love and affection. Of lust that blasts me out of my world into a space of a million crushed pieces that seem to mirror what I once was.

"Not like that, Nitu." My mother pins the sari *pallu* onto the shoulder of my blouse. It is yellow, a dark thick yellow that someone a hundred shades lighter than I should wear. Like Laila down the street with her bevy of suitors she rejects, inviting a flurry of who-does-she-think-she-is and does-she-think-she-will-find-a-good-husband-just-like-that-eh. My yellow sari brings out blotches on my face under the caking of too-white talcum powder and the pink lipstick framing my too-thin lips painted by my mother with a paintbrush as the women's magazines tell her to.

They are late, Prakrit and his parents, two hours late. By this time lines of sweat run ragged down my face. The potato and brinjal *bhajjias* lie desiccated on the center table, the chai is cold and skinned with cream, my mother is silent for once, my father reads the same page of the newspaper in his favorite chair, over and over again. I can sense them thinking, number seven, and this time he did not even come to see our daughter. I do not tell them of meeting Prakrit at work. If I had, my mother will now be imagining all kinds of things—sex, conception perhaps, daughter's reputation ruined.

Laila's mother comes, all clucks and concern, so sorry, they did not come, so sorry to hear that. All smiles. Her Laila says that the boy's side must respect us too. Such ideas, but she is so beautiful, only a matter of time before she goes from us to a big and rich house. Perhaps, and she hesitates delicately, and we must know how this is torn from her, how unwillingly she says this, but Nitu is so much like her own Laila, and so she will force herself to say to Nitu what she would say to her own daughter. Perhaps my mother and father should look . . . a little lower. America-return boy may be too high. For Nitu's good.

Five minutes after she leaves, Prakrit and his parents come. My mother calls out to them aloud, loud enough for the street to hear. She leans out into the sunshine hoping Laila's mother has not reached her house yet.

We twitter around them, as my mother blooms again. Prakrit's mother does not smile; she is dour, assessing, her eyes cold. She does not have to smile to please; she has an America-return son for sale. There are many buyers.

I am deeply in love, uncaring how ill-mannered his mother is. I know it will be Prakrit and with him America and dollars. How I do not know. I just know. My mother, so anxious to please, lies that I made the *bhajjias* and boiled the chai and pounded the cloves and cinnamon with my own two hands.

Prakrit and I do not look at each other. We are very solemn. I keep my eyes down, demure and bridelike; he talks intelligently with my father, filling our little drawing room with his so-American twang. I am in love.

The wedding takes place one week later. My mother comes into my room the night before I am to be married, sits on my bed, and stutters. I hear vague words, woman's duty, never deny your husband, touch his feet, rise before him, have his coffee ready when he wakes up, never raise your voice at him. She leaves, having satisfied herself that she has done her job as a mother in preparing me for a marriage that must last my whole life, unsaid, even in this modern age, is that if Prakrit (God forbid) dies, I must still keep faithful to his memory. A husband comes only once in a lifetime. All this, my mother teaches me in those fifteen minutes the night before I marry.

We honeymoon in Goa. The sun bleaches the sands to salt white, deepens the blue of the Arabian Sea. We sit under palm leaf–thatched umbrellas, go for walks at dusk. Prakrit searches out Australians and Americans and British and Dutch and French and speaks to them over drinks at the bar. They laugh together, the foreigners happy to find someone who speaks English a little like they do, Prakrit missing his job and his home in the Unied States. At night, he does things to me that excite me. And repulse me.

For two months I do not answer the phone. And when I do, if I hear Sheela's voice on the other end, I put it down. I am filled with loathing. I am filled with want. Nights I lie awake, listening to Prakrit's heavy breathing, and think she is six floors below. When she calls, the way she says my name sets me shaking. When she kissed me I did not pull away, did not scream in outrage. I kissed her back.

But how did I not know this about myself? All of my friends growing up were girls—we played together, slept in the same bed at times, kissed on the cheeks at others. We swooned over the same film star. Nothing in my life has prepared me for this. I was told that I would grow up to marry, to have children. I saw this all around me. I saw nothing else, I read of nothing like this as a child, or watched it in a movie. I know now, of course, have known for a few years, since I married and stepped out of the cocoon of my childhood home. And yet . . . I did not know this of *myself.*

I wander around the flat after the children and Prakrit are gone, dusting the tables and curios. A green plastic Statue of Liberty Prakrit got from his New York trip. The photo next to it is of him standing in front of the statue. A smattering of rain on the camera lens blurs his face. I polish my silver teapot and six cups that came as part of my dowry. I buff the wood *almirah* where I keep my saris and Prakrit's suits, also part of my dowry. The dining table, the chairs, the sofa, the carpet, all came from my parents. Prakrit's mother brought a list during the meeting before the wedding. They gave my parents three days to get all this together, before the ceremony. Or else.

There are other photos on the walls. Us together at Goa. I am wearing a *salwar kameez,* Prakrit looks grim and red-eyed, weeping from a gust of sand in his eyes. But on the whole we look happy. Then I was thinking of four more days with Prakrit before he returns to the United States. We register our wedding and Prakrit sends the papers to the American embassy for my visa. He is so solicitous, so caring. This is what marriage is supposed to be, where he will take care of me. Laila's mother is shattered with envy that the dark girl down the street is going to America to live. That she will come back maybe once a year with a trunk full of perfumy soaps and shampoos, that my mother will flaunt these smells when they meet. That I will slowly, over the years, say *heere* and call myself Neetoo.

The phone rings. I know who it is. This time I pick it up.

"Nitu." Her voice is soft. "Please don't hang up. Please."

I wait. I am trembling, suddenly longing to hear more of her voice.

"I'm sorry," she says.

I shake my head. As though she is at fault. We both . . . we both. But she cannot see me, of course.

"Let me come to see you. I can take an hour off at lunch."

"Why?"

"Let me come," she says.

I put the phone down carefully and go and sit on the sofa, my sofa. One of the things I can claim in this flat, and my parents gave it to me.

The noon hour passes slowly. Each time I hear the lift doors open, I think it is her. Each time I stand, waiting for the doorbell to ring. I see her face in my mind. See her smile. Ache for that kiss. Then I know she is not coming, that somehow, in talking to her, I have driven her away.

At four o' clock the children return home. They eat what

I make for them, they drink their milk. They go into their rooms and shut the doors, the flat is empty again. I wait for Prakrit. Every day these last two months he comes home and says, Ashok got promoted, Vivek got promoted, Shekar is going to the United States—this last with a shameful downward glance. We do not talk much of America anymore, not after . . .

The last four days we are to spend together after the honeymoon pass, then another four, and four weeks. Prakrit is still in India. We live with his parents, two kilometers from my parents' house. My mother asks when he is going; she does this in soft whispers when he is not present. I ask him too, but get no real response. Soon, he says, when his visa comes through. There is some problem. Then he tells me he is changing jobs, so the new company has to process his papers. I wonder about my own visa, but I am not to worry, he will take care of everything.

The longer we stay in India, the more Laila's mother starts to smile. She comes to visit my mother often, with news of Laila's marriage to a boy from a very good family, much land and property in India and—the final insult to my mother—he studied for his MS degree in America and works for a software company. The months pass, Laila marries and leaves almost immediately for California. Her first parcel to her mother contains three bottles of perfume with bold-sounding names, all of which smudge the air in our house after Laila's mother's visits. Finally, six months after the wedding, Prakrit tells me the truth.

His visa had expired long before he came back to India to get married. There is no chance of his returning, but his parents would not let that become common knowledge before the wedding. It would have wrecked their claims to Prakrit's eligibility, and demolished the dowry he could command. There is little I can do about the lies. At the beginning I am furious, but my father tells me to go back to my husband and not make any trouble, it was hard enough to get me married. I do. Prakrit looks for a job, and finds one on a probationary status in Mumbai. I am glad to move away from the city where I lived all my life to the anonymity and crowds of Mumbai. Fourteen years ago.

Prakrit comes home, pounding on the doorbell as usual. He looks tired and goes to sit at the table without a glance. He drinks his chai, eats his *pakoras,* asks where Sunny and Dinesh are. I watch in silence. He talks. Something about another promotion for someone else, not him.

"That color does not suit you," he says.

I look down at the yellow *salwar-kameez* I am wearing. I fan the chiffon *dupatta* over my dark fingers. I am suddenly angry. For years he has told me what to wear, how to wear it, how to sit and talk. As though he lives inside my skin. For years I have let him do this. Because there is no other way. Because this is all I have, or so I have been taught. In the end, it comes down to this. If not an America-return boy, at least one who is fair of skin, who has a job, whose job gives us this flat in Mumbai. But it no longer seems enough. Ten, twenty years from now I see us at this table. The children are gone to their own homes and families. I see us sitting here in silence. I see Prakrit telling me, as my hair grays and wrinkles map my face, what to wear.

"It suited me fine when you came to view me," I say.

He smiles. "No, it did not. But I had already decided to marry you, so the color did not matter."

"Why, Prakrit?" I ask. "Why did you marry me? There were others you could have chosen from." It is the first time I have questioned the lie, and his face reddens in rage.

"Let me see if I can explain it to you in terms you will understand, Nitu," he says, leaning back in his chair with a grin. "I had to choose—my parents and I had to choose— a girl without brothers who would kick up a fuss when I didn't return to the United States, and a father who would ignore her. When did your father ever look up from that damned newspaper that he reads in his chair each day to see what was happening around him?"

"What a bastard you are, Prakrit," I say.

He raises his eyebrows. "Don't talk too much, Nitu. Where are Sunny and Dinesh? Why haven't they come to say hello to me?"

He turns away, already dismissive.

"I'm leaving, Prakrit."

His head whips around. "Where are you going? To visit your parents? Not this month. Perhaps later."

Even this is familiar. He does not want me here because he *wants* me here. But because I am a fixture in this flat. A wife. A symbol of status.

"I'm not coming back."

His eyes grow cold. "What?"

I am too tired to talk, to give explanations. And he is not worth it. A few minutes ago the music from Sunny's room stopped, and she stands in the corridor, chewing that omnipresent gum. Dinesh hides behind her, his gaze steady on the two of us.

"What will you do, Nitu? Where will you go, to your parents? They will never take you back."

This I know. My mother would be horrified and I will be told my shadow must never again fall across their front door. This I know. I am terrified, molten with fear, but so determined. So sure I must do this so twenty years from now I do not sit across the table from him. So I can live.

I put my hand out to the children and they come with a confidence they have never before shown in me. Sunny comes to beyond my shoulders, yet she leans her head on my chest. Dinesh puts his arms around my waist. I am almost suffocated by his grip.

"Get out," Prakrit says. "Get the fucking hell out." His voice is triumphant. Because he thinks I will be coming back.

Sunny clutches at my *dupatta,* wiping her nose on it as she used to when she was a baby. We move together to the front door, open it. I stand there looking at Prakrit, but he is pouring himself a whiskey from the sideboard, another requirement on the list his mother gave my parents. It took our carpenter two days to make and cost more than my wedding saris. As we stand there, Prakrit comes up to us, and with one hand pushes us out just beyond the door. Then he shuts it gently. I hear him say, "Don't come back until you are ready to beg forgiveness. On your hands and knees."

I stand in the little landing with the three flat doors branching out. The lift light comes on and the door opens. Sheela steps out. She looks at us standing there, the children sticking to my side. Then she opens her arms. Sunny and Dinesh fly to her. I wonder why, they don't even know her. But they step into her circle of warmth. She lifts Dinesh and straddles him on one hip. He is heavy. He is eight, not a child anymore, but now he suddenly is.

I am crying. Tears drench the collar of my *kameez,* my nose runs.

"Come," Sheela says. "Come."

I stare at her. How did this happen? How did one day's worth of emotions, two months ago, change my whole life? How will we shatter two families, shatter every social code and more we have known? How?

"Come," she says again.

I go.

Afterword

A few years ago, *Seattle* magazine, our local monthly, called for submissions for its second annual fiction competition. One of their (not unreasonable) conditions was that the story have some "Seattle" connection, either in setting, or characters who once found their homes here, or *something*—they were very generous.

Having decided to submit for the competition, for the first time in my writing career I had to write a story to fit a specific theme and a market. This Seattle story of mine wasn't an easy task, for the simple reason that until then all my fiction—novels and short stories—had been set in India. I had completed both *The Twentieth Wife* and *The Feast of Roses,* both set in seventeenth-century Mughal India, and had written numerous contemporary short stories, drawing on my experiences from my childhood and college years. It was a daunting task, all of a sudden. I had no wish then (and now) to write about the immigrant Indian experience—I was living the life and didn't feel I had lived it long enough to sit back, draw a breath, and view my experiences with a writer's eye, from all sides, prejudiced and not.

I began and let waste a couple of short stories because they were going nowhere; the characters seemed flat, the voice insipid, the plot sluggish. When the weekend came around, my husband and I went to dinner at an Indian friend's home. At the table, our hostess began a story about one of her colleagues at work. My friend's colleague had just received a call from her sister in Belgium, married to a Belgian man, who had adopted a little girl from India (actually the city of Chennai) some twenty-odd years ago. A few days before, a letter had come to them from the orphanage at Chennai, with the request that the girl come back to India to see her mother who was dying. The Belgian parents, and their now-Belgian daughter, had not returned to India after the adoption and knew no Indians at all. So the mother's phone call to her sister (and my friend's colleague) in Seattle was to ask her to find out from my friend if she thought if the letter was legitimate, if they should indeed go to see this woman who had given up her child to the orphanage . . . if . . .

My friend has a mobile face and a rhythm to her voice, especially suited for storytelling. She can mimic and mime, be grave and irreverent in turn, but I was, at best, a preoccupied audience that evening. The dinner ended, we went home and to bed, and I worried myself to sleep. The next morning, I awoke and began to write "Shelter of Rain."

I wrote steadily over the next three days, let the story rest for another three, and revised for another three days before I sent it in to *Seattle* magazine. A few weeks later, they returned the story to me with thanks and their regrets—they had decided to cancel their second annual fiction competition. All that fretting for nothing! But I still had my Seattle story, after all.

Sometime before this, I had picked up a copy of *India Today,* India's weekly news magazine, at the local library and remember staring at the cover picture for a long while—it was a photo of a gray-haired man and woman lying on the concrete pavement where they had fallen. They looked peaceful, almost asleep, faces turned to the side, but a ribbon of blood zigzagged out from the man's head onto the concrete. When I eventually turned to the accompanying article, it was to read about (my) Meha and Chandar and their son, (my) Bikaner, and how they had flung themselves from the balcony of their flat to stop their son's abuse. Neighbors said that it was because the son wanted the flat they owned in Mumbai. This is about all of what I remember from the article.

It took me months of thinking about Meha and Chandar and Bikaner, of who they were, where they came from, why . . . why . . . why . . . before I could write "Three and a Half Seconds."

From the first writing of the story, I had structured it

around the jump, and my initial title, chosen for no reason, was "Nine and a Half Seconds." Optimistically, as it turned out. With a great deal of help (such terminology not being part of my normal vocabulary), I calculated the coefficient of friction for a falling human body, the drag (or lack of it, since it was warm weather and they would not have been clad in cumbersome clothing), whether they would reach terminal velocity (no, not enough of a height), a more reasonable distance for them to fall (from the sixteenth floor), and the title was pared down to "Three and a Half Seconds." This is one of my early stories—I think it might predate all the stories in this collection—but it is the most difficult story I have written.

Most Indian readers will probably recognize the premise of "The Faithful Wife." I read this story of a Sati in my local newspaper, while drinking my coffee, just before leaving for college in the late 1980s. It was a little article, tucked away into a corner reserved for late-breaking news as the paper is being put to bed for the night. Since, of course, the Deorala Sati and Roop Kanwar have been written about, discussed, and analyzed. But I wrote "The Faithful Wife" from that one memory of that little article, so my facts (my fiction, really) aren't accurate (and they aren't meant to be), other than the fact of the Sati taking place. I remembered that a reporter had arrived at Deorala the morning after, and this reporter (my Ram) became the focus of "The Faithful Wife." What would he have done if he had arrived just before the event? What would he have done if his grandparents lived in the village—if they were somehow complicit in the Sati?

There is some background, such as these, in all the stories of *In the Convent of Little Flowers*. A tale told over dinner, an article read in a newspaper, even a much-forwarded email with a "can you believe this is happening in *India*?" as in the case of "The Key Club." Everything triggers a thought, some thinking; sometimes this develops into a story, if I can find enough of a motivation and conjure up a history. Sometimes, as in the case of "The Chosen One," I set out to write another story and this is what I ended up with.

It's easier to cram only craziness and eccentricity in a short story rather than a novel—there it would be simply exhausting. Novels need lulls, breathing spaces. In the short story, the lull comes afterward, when the story has been read and put away and there is time for reflection. So if there's one thing the stories have in common, it is that they all deal with that intense moment in which people confront disturbing events in their lives. I didn't put these stories together with a theme in mind, and there is none really, I think, other than perhaps my reminiscences, old and new, of my homeland.

Indu Sundaresan
January 2008

Acknowledgments

$\mathcal{T}$his collection was created over a period of some years; consequently, I've shown the stories, in one avatar or another, to members of my critique groups. Thank you, for your thoughts, questions and comments, which have helped shape these stories into their current form.

My agent, Sandy Dijkstra, has a steady and wise guiding hand, and everyone at the Sandra Dijkstra Literary Agency is brilliant and efficient—it's such a pleasure working with all of you.

It has been awhile, eight years or so, but I still remember that stunning happiness on hearing that Judith Curr, my publisher at Atria Books, had agreed to publish my first novel. I've worked with Malaika Adero, my editor at Atria Books, only a few years less, and I'm grateful to both of you for your support and encouragement, especially with this book, which is something new from my pen. My deepest thanks also to the Copyediting Department at Atria (for stellar copyediting), the Art Department (for spectacular covers), and the Publicity Department (for believing in my work and championing it to the outside world).

To Uday and Sitara: just this; you make all of this, and indeed everything else in my life, worthwhile.

Finally, a note to readers around the world, who have written in to keep me company with their stories and had kind words of praise for mine—I appreciate your letters more than I can express.

Readers Club Guide

In the
Convent
of
Little Flowers

Introduction

*I*n this collection of stories, celebrated author Indu Sundaresan departs from her body of historical novels to explore themes of significance to Indians today. These nine works of short fiction tell the stories of contemporary Indians challenged by ancient traditions and culture, struggling to find a place and a way of life in a world that offers some women more opportunities than ever while denying others even the most basic freedoms. With Sundaresan's trademark lush prose, vividly rendered settings, complex and appealing characters, and compelling narratives, *In the Convent of Little Flowers* illuminates the lives of Indian women living at home and abroad, embracing and rejecting modern lives.

Questions and Topics for Discussion

1. In "Shelter of Rain," why is Padmini so angry to hear from Sister Mary Theresa, the woman who practically raised her until her adoption at age six? What reasons does the nun give Padmini for her mother's abandonment and neglect? How does Padmini feel about those reasons? Do you sympathize with her mother at all?

2. Indian culture has long emphasized the importance of respect for elders, particularly with regard to aging parents. In "Three and a Half Seconds" and "Bedside Dreams," we witness the devastating effects of the rejection of this tradition. Why do Meha and Chandar ultimately choose death over asking for help or standing up to their cruel son, Bikaner? What does "Bedside Dreams" say about the effect of Western culture on young Indians with elderly parents? Do you think the nameless narrator and her husband, Kamal, did in fact

"go wrong" raising their twelve children to be cast off so readily?

3. Compare and contrast the way Payal's grandmother in "Fire" and Kamal and his wife in "Bedside Dreams" are treated. Describe the situations these elderly characters face at the end of their lives and explain how they got there. Do you think they deserve their fates? Why or why not?

4. Banyan trees appear in several of the stories in this collection. Identify which stories this symbol appears in and discuss the ways in which the characters use the banyan tree. What do you think the tree symbolizes?

5. Though not all of the narrators in this story are women, the stories do seem to center on one or several women's experiences. What do these stories tell you about the traditional roles of women in Indian culture? What is expected of women in their roles as daughters, sisters, wives, and mothers? How do you feel about these expectations?

6. The idea of an arranged marriage often seems cruel to modern minds and hearts. But these stories portray another side. What are the benefits of an arranged marriage as experienced by the characters of *In the Convent of Little Flowers*? What are some of the detriments?

7. In "The Faithful Wife," we follow a reporter back to the small rural village of his birth, where a twelve-year-old

girl is about to be burned alive in the ancient (outlawed) tradition of Sati. Does the issue of Western encroachment upon Indian traditions drive the conflict here, or is this an example of age-old sexism mediated by evolved opinion? What do you think of Ram's observation (page 58) that the villagers perform the Sati with "a vicious need to connect with the past, with a willing scapegoat"?

8. Why do the members of the Key Club stop seeing one another outside of their meetings? Why do they use false names, even though some of them have been friends since childhood? What does it mean to Ram that his wife, Sita, avoid choosing Sat as her mate, and how does this relate to her repeated choice of Vish? Do you think Ram is missing something important in this story?

9. Using these stories as examples, discuss the ways in which Western values and concepts have infiltrated and affected Indian culture. What aspects are new to India? What aspects have always been present, but are newly exposed by changing perspectives and ideas of what is acceptable?

10. In "The Most Unwanted," Nathan struggles with feelings of shame and betrayal. His daughter has committed the ultimate sin—giving birth to a bastard and remaining unmarried. What is it that ultimately begins to heal the dull ache and bitter pain inside his chest?

11. In "Fire," Payal says her grandmother "hides behind a strange and immovable logic" (page 88). Identify the ways in which this statement applies to other characters in the collection. Discuss what this really means and what effect, both positive and negative, this stance has on each story.

12. While many of these stories portray tragic lives with even more tragic endings, there is happiness found among the pages of this collection, too. Where do the women of *In the Convent of Little Flowers* find happiness? Compare and contrast these sources of joy with the ways in which modern Western women find happiness.

13. Which story did you most identify with and why? Do you think the challenges these women face are universal? Why or why not?

Enhance Your
Book Club Experience

1. Several of the stories in this collection address the benefits and detriments of arranged marriages, an ancient tradition in India. Not only is this tradition still practiced by modern Indians, it is also currently practiced by several other cultures, including modern Asian cultures and some Jewish sects—both at home and among those members who have transplanted to the United States. Do a little reading about modern arranged marriages and share your findings with your book club. You can start at www.huffingtonpost.com/tag/arranged-marriage.

2. The preparation and serving of certain foods and drinks plays a central, if subtle, role in the Indian households portrayed in these stories. Get into the mood by preparing some for yourself—better yet, make your next book club meeting an Indian buffet! There are many Indian cookbooks available, and the internet offers a host of

recipe collections (check out www.indianfoodrecipes .net). If you don't quite feel up to cooking, seek out the nearest Indian restaurant and try something from the menu.

3. Though movies aren't necessarily reliable sources of information, they can provide a peek into foreign cultures and ways of thinking that is very effective for Western viewers. Try renting a few "Bollywood" movies or Hollywood movies about modern Indians (such as *Bend It Like Beckham*) and watch them with your book club.

4. Author Indu Sundaresan has previously written historical novels that take place in ancient India. Try reading a few to see how her characters in the past compare to her portrayal of characters living in modern times. You can also learn more about Sundaresan by visiting her website at www.indusundaresan.com.